The Story of the Blue Planet

ANDRI SNÆR MAGNASON

Illustrated by
ÁSLAUG JÓNSDÓTTIR
Translated by
JULIAN MELDON D'ARCY

PUSHKIN CHILDREN'S BOOKS

The Story of the Blue Planet

Pushkin Children's Books
71-75 Shelton Street, London WC2H 9JQ

Copyright © 1999 by Andri Snær Magnason
Illustration copyright © 1999 by Áslaug Jónsdóttir
English translation © 2012 by Julian Meldon D'Arcy

Title of the original Icelandic edition: *Sagan af bláa hnettinum*
Published by agreement with Forlagið, www.forlagid.is

First published in the US by Seven Stories Press, New York
First published in the UK by Pushkin Press

ISBN 978 1 782690 06 1

The translation of this book was made possible
with a grant from the Icelandic Literature Fund.

Bókmenntasjóður
The Icelandic Literature Fund

Printed and bound in Italy by Printer Trento SRL
on Munken Print White 100gsm

To my son, Hlynur, and his great grandparents

Contents

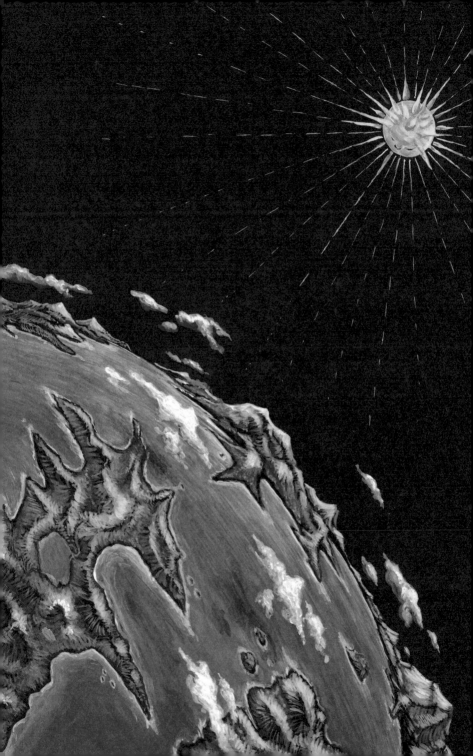

There Was a Blue Planet

Once upon a time there was a blue planet far out in space. At first sight, it looked like a very ordinary blue planet and it's unlikely that an astrologist or astronaut would even have given it a second glance. A sun and a moon circled the planet once every day and wind swayed the grass and flowers, while waterfalls tumbled from high mountains into deep dark canyons. Clouds were blown across the sky and stars twinkled behind them. The planet was covered with lands and around each land was an ocean that could be as calm as a mirror until it was caught by the roaring winds and smashed into a thousand drops on rocky shores.

The blue planet was very special for one reason: Only children lived there. Plants and animals lived there too of course, but all around the planet were children in all shapes and sizes. Big children, small children, chubby children, and skinny children, and some were even weird like the child you see in the mirror. There were many more than a hundred of them, so let's just say that they were countless. The children were completely free to do what they pleased since no grown-ups lived on the blue planet and there was no one to order them around. The wild children ate when they were hungry, slept when they got tired, and in between they played without anyone interfering. These words are not meant to criticize grown-ups; many of them are quite nice.

The blue planet was beautiful, but it was also a dangerous place. Each day was so full of danger and excitement that no grown-ups could have lived there without getting gray hair and withering away from stress and worry. That's why no grown-up had landed on the planet for as long as the youngest child could remember, and astronomers wouldn't dare point their telescopes towards the blue planet.

Now someone might ask: Where did the children come from? How did they multiply? Did they never grow up? How were they born if there were no grown-ups living on the planet? The answer is simple: Nobody knows.

As I said, scientists were not interested in the planet and no research had been done on it. We only know that it was full of children that never grew up. For some unknown reason the well of youth in their hearts seemed limitless, and in fact, the children could easily have been many hundreds of years old.

The children had endless adventures on the blue

planet. They could follow fireflies in the dark or climb rocky cliffs and jump into warm waters. They could gather shells on the beach and watch the sea turtles crawl ashore to lay their eggs. There were high cliffs full of nesting birds and cold white glaciers that crawled to the sea, crunching and crumbling. The forests were light-green during the day when the tigers and parrots were about, but they turned dark-green in the evening when the wolves began howling, and black-green at night when the bats awoke and spiders with hairy legs wove their webs between branches.

Once a year an incredible event took place on the blue planet. A ray of light would burst through a little hole in the wall of a cave in the Blue Mountains. This was no ordinary cave. It was full of sleeping butterflies. As the light flooded the cave and shone on their wings, something wonderful happened: the butterflies awoke

from their sleep. Very slowly and calmly they moved their wings and then rose in the air, one by one, and flew out of the mouth of the cave. They followed the sun for a whole day, circling the planet over land and sea, mountains and valleys, before fluttering back into the cave and falling asleep again, not to awaken until another year had passed.

The flight of the butterflies was the greatest wonder on the blue planet and a day of true happiness. The children would lie on their backs and watch the butterflies fill the sky until they disappeared with the sun beyond the horizon.

But all these wonders cannot compare with the adventure this story has to tell. Here comes the most dangerous and incredible adventure that any child on the blue planet could ever have imagined.

The Saga Begins

The saga begins on a little island in a deep ocean, shortly before the annual awakening of the butterflies. It was a bright summer's day and Brimir was wandering along a black sandy beach collecting seashells and skimming the ocean with flat stones. He walked slowly through the penguin nesting grounds, zigzagging through the crowd, taking special care not to step on any eggs.

Brimir was going to show his friend Hulda a beautiful stone he had found near the Blue Mountains. Only a glimpse of his head could be seen, as a lock of his yellow hair stood out among the black and white flock of penguins. His tummy was grumbling because he had completely forgotten to eat on his hike. He looked at the delicious eggs under the penguins' bottoms and his mouth watered, but when he caught their nasty looks he decided to let them be. After all, he was alone against thousands of them; he had a sharp mind but their beaks were sharper.

Brimir saw Hulda dragging a large sack and ran over to her.

"Hi," said Brimir. "What's in the sack?"

"Just a seal."

"Just a seal?"

"Yes, just one seal, but also oranges and two rabbits!"

"Mmmm! Did you catch the seal?"

"Oh, it was no big deal, it was so small. I knocked it out with a club," said Hulda as she tapped Brimir lightly on his head.

"Shall I help you pull the sack?"

"That would be nice."

Brimir and Hulda strolled along the beach, dragging the sack behind them, wiping out their tracks in the sand. They looked out over the sea and the black sand in the bay with the palm trees where they were going to skin and cook the seal. They collected logs, lit a fire, and grilled the seal in one piece. When they had eaten their fill they sat in the sand and watched the sunset. Then they lay on their backs and watched the stars grow brighter as the darkness grew blacker.

"I think this was the best and most beautiful day of my life," whispered Hulda.

"Yes, it's even better than the second-best day I've ever lived, which was yesterday," said Brimir.

"What did you do yesterday?"

"Nothing special. I just felt so happy," said Brimir, smiling. "Life keeps getting better and better."

"And the butterflies are coming soon," said Hulda, glowing with happiness.

Brimir showed Hulda the stone he found. How it glittered. Like a thousand rainbows. Like a million stars.

"It's beautiful!"

"You can have it," said Brimir.

"No, I don't want it," said Hulda, "it's too beautiful."

"Really, I want you to have it," said Brimir.

Knowing in her heart that it's a greater blessing to give than to receive, Hulda accepted the stone to please Brimir.

"What kind of stone is it?"

"I think it's a wishing stone."

"Can I make a wish?" asked Hulda.

"Yes, if you want to," replied Brimir, "but then the stone changes into an ordinary pebble."

"Do I only get the one wish?"

"Yes, but you can make whatever wish you like."

Hulda was silent. She thought things over, racked her brains, and let her mind wander.

"I really can't think of anything to wish for."

"Nothing?" asked Brimir.

"I have enough to eat and I have many friends because everybody's my friend. But there's always been one wish I've had," said Hulda.

"And what's that?"

"I've always wished that my best friend would give me an amazingly beautiful wishing stone. And now my wish has come true so I can't think of anything else to wish for!"

Hulda smiled shyly, kissed Brimir quickly on the cheek, and held the stone carefully, like a sparrow's egg.

"That's a really strange star!" said Brimir suddenly.

"Where?" asked Hulda.

"There!" shouted Brimir.

"There shouldn't be a star there," said Hulda and rubbed her eyes.

But the star was not motionless in space. It zoomed about with a large tail of fire, sometimes twisting and turning as it drew glowing letters of fire in the sky.

"It's making letters in the air," said Brimir.

"L-E-T T-H-E-R-E B-E F-U-N," spelled out Hulda.

"Let there be fun? What kind of falling star is that?"

The star suddenly stopped making circles in the air and now it was heading straight for the blue planet! A horrendous roar could be heard that became louder and louder. Brimir and Hulda clung to each other.

"Oh, no, is it an asteroid or a comet?"

"It's a space rocket! And it's going to crash!"

The space rocket approached with increasing speed and everything around them became blindingly bright. The birds in the trees flew away shrieking. Squirrels crawled into rabbit holes. Fish hid in seaweed forests.

Hulda shouted, "It's heading straight for us! We'll be crushed."

"Hold me tight," whispered Brimir.

Hulda held onto Brimir so tightly she almost crushed him. Then came a tremendous explosion.

BANG!

The explosion echoed between the mountains, while sand and rocks rained all over the beach.

Brimir and Hulda remained perfectly still with their ears ringing. A deep crater had been formed where the space rocket had crashed. They walked slowly to the crater's edge and peeked over. Hardly anything could be seen because of the smoke, but they caught a glint of a glowing, battered, shapeless wreck at the bottom.

"It's just like an old vacuum cleaner," said Hulda.

"It's a spaceship," whispered Brimir.

There was no sign of life in the spaceship, but then a low knocking sound could be heard—bang, wham, thump—as if someone was trying to break open the door of the rocket.

"No one's come here from outer space for ages," said Hulda.

The door continued to be struck, now much harder than before.

BANG! WHAM! THUMP!

"I hope it's not a space monster," whispered Brimir.

Then a dreadful roar could be heard and the door was struck with full force. It fell open with a loud crash and a gigantic dark creature appeared in the doorway. It stared out into the darkness.

The Space Monster

Brimir and Hulda ran through the night as fast as their legs could carry them to let their friends know about the space monster. Their only light was from the moon, which sometimes disappeared behind a cloud or a palm tree. They ran over meadows and through forests and along the river and over the desert. All the time they were shouting and calling:

"Beware of the space monster! A space monster's arrived!"

The children woke up and shouted terrified out into the darkness:

"Where's the space monster?"

"It's down on the beach with the black sand. RUN! HIDE!"

"What does the space monster look like?" some of them asked.

"I think it was black," shouted Hulda and she kept on running.

"Yes, it was black and hairy with four heads and its teeth were sharper than knives!" cried Brimir.

"Bread knives or meat knives?" called out Arnar the thinker.

"We're not sure, the space monster was really just black," cried Hulda pulling Brimir on behind her.

And before they were out of sight they shouted to the kids: "Don't go near the black beach!"

The news spread through the forest that night like wildfire and lit up fear in every heart. All the children had heard about the monster but few of them knew what it looked like. Some of them said that it was black and hairy and could swallow whole planets with forests and lakes and all the animals in one big mouthful. Others said it had ten heads and eighteen eyes with x-ray vision to see through mountains.

They all imagined the horror of disappearing into the stomach of such a monster and being crushed in its smelly and slimy guts. Brimir and Hulda, exhausted after their running, fell asleep in a forest glade under a sweet-scented pine tree.

Hulda was awoken by a terrified cry from Brimir.

"Oh, I had such a horrible nightmare! The space monster replaced our hearts with lots of feathers, which tickled so much that I couldn't stop laughing when the monster ate me and chewed me a hundred times because the monster's mother had taught it to chew its food very well, and finally, when the monster swallowed me, its belly was full of jellyfish jam. And you know how I hate jellyfish!"

Hulda shook her head. "You and your crazy, mixed-up dreams."

"I think we've slept too long," said Brimir rubbing his eyes. "Let's find the others before the monster eats us all."

The children walked for a long, long time through the forest. It was by now a bright sunny day, but there wasn't a single child in sight. There were no children by the river or up on the hills. There was no child in the valley or under the mountain. Brimir and Hulda shouted and called, but nobody answered except the monkeys in the trees and the rustling leaves.

"I think the monster's already eaten our friends," whimpered Brimir.

"I'll find the club I used to knock out the seal," said Hulda, "and I'll knock out the space monster."

Hulda swung her club and almost knocked out Brimir. They crept down to the black beach, where they heard a frightful noise.

"Hush, Hulda, what's that sound? Is that the noise a space monster makes when it cracks open skulls and sucks out the brains?"

"It sounds more like laughter to me," said Hulda.

"Oh, no!" shouted Brimir. "That means there isn't just one space monster but a whole bunch of horrible, laughing space monsters, more dangerous than all the wolves and all the lions and all the poisonous snakes put together!"

They crawled, trembling on hands and knees, up to the ridge of the crater and looked down to where the spaceship had crashed. An unbelievable sight awaited them.

Mr. Goodday

"What's that?" asked Brimir, amazed.

"The monster is like an overgrown child!" said Hulda, catching her breath.

"I think I know what it is," said Brimir. "It could be a grown-up, they're supposed to be gigantic."

This grown-up man also appeared to be hilarious, for all around him sat most of their friends laughing their heads off! They were all looking at this amazing creature sitting on top of a twisted space rocket. He was wearing a Hawaiian shirt with a gray briefcase in his hand. He certainly did not look like a space monster.

"Are grown-ups dangerous?" asked Brimir.

"Some of them are very dangerous, but this one just seems to be funny," said Hulda.

Brimir and Hulda breathed easier, but still looked a little embarrassed. The extremely dangerous space monster was just a very funny man. They crept down into the crater to join the children.

Brimir sat by his friend Magni who was bursting with laughter.

"Who is he?" asked Brimir.

"Ssh! Just listen."

"Hello, kids. My name is Gleesome Goodday and I'm the most *way*-out guy in the world and I can do **ANYTHING**, let me tell you, because I'm the coolest man who has ever set foot on this blue planet!"

Mr. Goodday handed out his card among the children.

Gleesome Goodday

Stardust vacuum cleaner traveling salesman

but chiefly

Dream**ComeTrueMaker and joybringer**

Sell phone: 763-8381-9599-9383-8993-3444
Spaced phone: 160-5070-5855-5589-3453
Outofsite: www.goodday.mm.is

"A dream-come-true-maker?"

"A Stardust vacuum cleaner traveling salesman?"

"Wow, that's a weird job," said Hulda.

"You are all so unbelievably lucky to have been chosen for a **special** *offer*," cried Mr. Goodday. "I am going make your sweetest dreams come true!"

"Are dreams not true?" asked Arnar the thinker.

"When you fall asleep at night the dreams wake up. They crawl through your ears like little bugs and walk inside your brain and tell you strange stories all night. Sometimes the stories are so amusing that you don't want to wake. But sometimes they are so terrifying that you'd rather never fall asleep again. I know how to make your dreams come true."

"Are you sure that dreams can come true?" asked Brimir. "Mine are so weird."

The children looked at Brimir and laughed. He had often told them of his dreams in the morning and they were truly amazing.

"Like the dream of the flying penguins and the nightmare about the screaming trees," said Hulda and laughed.

Mr. Goodday looked over the group of children and smiled.

"What's your name, young man?"

"My name's Brimir."

"Well, what are we waiting for Brimir? I'll start by changing you into a flying penguin."

Mr. Goodday turned to Brimir and waved his arms around.

"Dreamacadabra, a flying penguin you shall be . . ."

The children watched in amazement while Brimir closed his eyes and waited for whatever would happen. But Mr. Goodday just laughed and did a reverse somersault off the spaceship.

"I was just joking! I make your most wildest dreams come true, not your weirdest, and so make life a hundred times better."

The kids giggled.

"Do you want to make life better? Then you're really on the wrong planet. We think life is great! It can't get any better."

"Let's see," said Mr. Goodday. "What's the greatest fun you can think of?"

Magni answered first.

"When the moon is full I go to the high cliffs with my bird-net and listen to the wind and the waves. I sit on the edge of the cliff and wait for the bats to crawl out of their holes and glide around in the moonlight and suck the blood out of the seals sleeping on the rocks below. Then I catch a few bats with my net and roast them on a fire and make hats from their wings."

"I like climbing to the top of mountains and looking out over the land, but I most want to climb the Blue Mountains," said Ragnar, and looked dreamily into the distance.

"When the rain pours down from the sky we can swing through the trees and jump down into muddy puddles, and when I'm splattered up to my neck I can go and wash myself clean in the misty spray from the waterfall," said Elva smiling.

And so the children continued, on and on, until they heard a tremendous yawn.

It was from Mr. Goodday.

"Oh, I do beg your pardon, dear kids, but this was all so dreadfully dull and boring that I almost fell asleep. Don't you really know how to have a good time?"

The children looked at each other in surprise.

"But that is having a good time!"

"Yeah, we think so!"

"No, no, I'm talking about real fun and games," said Mr. Goodday. "Oh dear, you're all so horribly underdeveloped."

There was silence for a little while, and then suddenly Hulda lit up.

"We forgot the most best thing of all, guys! When the butterflies wake up in the cave and follow the sun. That's real fun because it's the most beautiful thing that ever happens in the world!"

"After the flight of the butterflies we're so happy that our happiness lasts a whole year, right until the butterflies fly again. Then we're out of this world with joy!"

Mr. Goodday yawned again.

"What do you know of the world? Okay, so there are beautiful butterflies, fine. But I can show you things much cooler and even more **fun** than all of what you've said put together, all at a special-terms, special-offer price with a sales discount!"

"Cooler and more fun?"

"At a special-terms, special-offer price?"

"Yes, that's right, with a sales discount!"

"But nothing costs anything here," said Magni.

"I'm quite sure you'll want to pay for this," said Mr. Goodday smiling over the group. He looked straight into the eyes of every single child.

"Do you want to fly? Free as birds? Light as a butterfly?"

Butterfly Powder

Mr. Goodday knew that everyone dreamed of flying like a bird or a butterfly over mountains and wilderness. Even old women with a fear of heights wake up with their hearts full of joy after such a dream.

Brimir answered for the children.

"Of course we want to fly like butterflies. At night we dream countless dreams in which we fly and glide, and they're the most enjoyable dreams we have. But we know it's impossible because of gravity."

"Are you trying to trick us?" asked Hulda looking searchingly at Mr. Goodday.

"No, I'm not trying to trick you. I really do know a way to let you fly."

The kids looked at each other skeptically.

"Could we really get to fly in the air like the birds?"

"Show me where the butterflies sleep and you shall fly. That's a promise, and not a lie."

The children had butterflies in their tummies. Could they really fly? They set off in single row through the forest, along the river, over the hills, and through the valley until they came to the cave in the mountain

where the butterflies sleep for a whole year
after following the sun around the planet.

"Hush!" whispered the children. "We
mustn't wake the butterflies."

"Is this the butterfly cave?" shouted Mr.
Goodday, peeping through the opening.

"Yes, the butterflies sleep here."

Mr. Goodday took a large vacuum
cleaner out of his case.

"This is an AP XU 456r 2000 Super
Vacuum Cleaner."

"Won't it wake the butterflies?"

"Vacuum cleaners are silent, don't you
know anything?" asked Mr. Goodday in
amazement.

He connected a long tube to the machine and stuck it
through the cave mouth. He turned the machine on—
and it was true, it made no sound at all.

"Are you sucking up the butterflies?" asked Brimir,
growing pale.

"There are no laws in this island so it must be okay to
vacuum-clean butterflies."

"Are you vacuuming up the butterflies?" asked the
children, terrified.

"My goodness, how you all get so worked up! Have a
look in the cave."

The kids looked into the cave and saw all the floors

and walls and rocks were covered with butterflies fast asleep, just as usual. They all sighed with relief.

Mr. Goodday opened the vacuum cleaner, took the dust-bag out and held it up high.

"Do you know what's in this bag?"

The children looked at each other.

"Stardust?"

"Butterfly poop?"

"No, it's the most unbelievable magic powder in the world, my dears. It's BUTTERFLY POWDER!"

"Butterfly powder?"

"Have you never caught a butterfly?"

They had all caught a butterfly at one time or another.

"When you let it go isn't the palm of your hand some-times covered by a glittering dust?"

"Yes," said the children.

"That's the powder that makes the butterflies fly when the sun shines on their wings."

"And what are we supposed to do with this butterfly powder?" asked the children.

"I'll show you."

Mr. Goodday walked over to Magni and sprinkled the powder over his hands. At first nothing happened, but then it was as if he was becoming light as a feather, and then, suddenly, he floated up off the ground and hov-ered over their heads. The children caught their breaths in amazement.

"I'm flying! I'm flying!" shouted Magni.

The kids on the ground burst into laughter.

"He's flying!" they shouted, laughing and dancing.

"I'm flying!" Magni shouted. "This is the greatest fun I've ever had!"

He glided in the air like a bird. He flew in circles, did a few dives, and his tummy tingled with excitement. He hung onto branches, took kiwi fruits and oranges from the tops of trees, and threw them down to the others.

"This is fantastic. This is just unbelievably fantastic. This is unbelievable, stupendous fun! Mr. Goodday is the jolliest man in the world!" he shouted.

"Now we'll call him nothing else but Jolly-Goodday!" cried Hulda.

"Hooray for Jolly-Goodday!" the children all shouted as one.

"How much does the butterfly powder cost?"

"Nothing, my dear children. You can have it for free."

"Hooray!"

The children gathered and jostled round Jolly-Goodday, and from the crowd could be heard shouts and cries of "May I? Me next! Then me! Me too!" And they all received butterfly powder on their arms.

"We're free like butterflies!" shouted the children.

Brimir and Hulda glided hand in hand all round the island that day. They saw places no child had ever seen before. They saw spring waters in the forest where the green crocodiles lay white eggs. They flew over hidden valleys between glaciers with dinosaur bones, and they could look straight down into a volcanic crater with its bubbling lava.

Hulda sat on the crater's edge and stared into the melted rocks. She could feel the burning heat. Brimir sat next to her, picked up a large pebble, and threw it into the crater. The stone melted and became floating lava. Hulda tied some string around a chunk of seal meat from the previous day and lowered it down into the crater. The chunk was cooked in an instant and they drew it up grilled and juicy from the fire.

"There's one thing I'd like to see," said Hulda, munching on her meat.

"What's that?" asked Brimir, licking his fingers.

"I want to see the lions."

Brimir's eyes brightened and his heart beat faster. He had only once seen a lion from a great distance, and had never dared go near them. They glided off to the great plain where a pride of lions lay at ease under an oak tree, bad-tempered male lions, with bloody teeth and great manes, and some fierce lionesses, with cute little cubs playing all around them. The children circled over the tree and perched like sparrows on a branch. The lions stood up and growled.

GRRRROWL!!!

"Ha, ha! You can't get me!" cried Brimir as he threw acorns at the lions.

GRRRROWL!!!

"Eat me if you can!" said Hulda growling back.

Their hearts pounded faster when the biggest lion with the biggest mane gripped the bark with its claws and inched its way up the tree. They had often heard horrible stories of lions that devoured every last morsel of a child and left nothing behind but a gnawed skeleton in the grass.

"Let's fly away now," said Brimir.

"Not just yet."

"Does the powder ever stop working?"

"Not while the sun's shining."

The lion clawed itself higher and higher up the tree. It growled so ferociously that the leaves paled and the berries fell to the ground.

GRRRROWL!!!

The lion sprang onto the branch just below the children as a cloud was fast approaching the sun.

"Quick," said Hulda, "let's fly away!"

They flapped up into the air and left the lion completely baffled in the tree.

"GRR! What kind of creatures are you anyway?"

"We're flying penguins," cried Brimir, and he burst out laughing. "This is more fun than the weirdest dream!"

They flew away laughing over lakes and forests, mountains and rivers.

Ragnar the mountain-climber flew up all the mountaintops on the island before he let his most treasured dream come true and flew twice to the peak of the Blue Mountains and then down again.

"Wow, this was the best day of my life," he shouted. "It was fantastic!"

"Yeah, the next most fun day is really dull and boring compared to this one," said Brimir.

"I don't understand how we could have ever lived without this fantastic butterfly powder," said Hulda with the broadest of smiles.

Evening Falls, the Sun Sets

But the butterfly powder only worked while the sun shone, and when the sun began to set the children's flying powers grew weaker until they were as heavy and earthbound as they had been before. The children rushed backwards and forwards like wing-clipped birds, some flapping their arms and hopping in the air.

"Oh, it's so boring when the sun has set and the sky becomes red in the west and black in the east," said Elva before she jumped off a low ledge and crashed onto a pile of rocks.

"I think so too," said Magni, pouting. "You stop having butterflies in your tummy and you're as heavy as lead and can't fly anymore. It's terribly boring."

"It's so tiring to walk," said Ragnar.

"I think it's so boring to sleep," said Elva. "Our dreams are colorless compared to the fun we have during the day."

The next day, the very same thing happened all over again: the kids flew and glided and laughed themselves silly, but when the sun set they all became very moody and silent, each sitting alone, waiting for the sun to rise again. No one could be bothered to sleep because the reality of the day had become so much more fun than the dreams of the night.

At last the children decided to go down to Black Beach and ask Jolly-Goodday if he could make the butterfly powder work at night as well. It was very early in the morning and the sun had hardly risen. Jolly-Goodday slept under a woollen blanket on a deck chair on the beach. He had sleep in his eyes and hair on his toes. He yawned when the children woke him.

"YAWN," he yawned. "What do you all want?"

"The nights are so dull," the children complained.

Jolly-Goodday was very understanding.

"Do you find your dreams unexciting?"

"Yeah, sleeping is so dull and boring, we want to fly at night too. You have to find a way."

Jolly-Goodday thought deeply, mulled things over, and racked his brains so much he almost split his mind in two.

"I'm sure I can fix it, and it won't cost much at all."

"Hooray, hooray!" shouted the children. "Jolly-Goodday knows everything! How much will it cost?"

"Really nothing at all and less than that."

"How little?"

"Maybe just a tiny bit of youth."

"Youth?"

"In your hearts there's a very deep well that waters your soul and it's full to the brim of youth."

"Are you going to take our youth?"

"No, no, no. Not all of it, just a tiny little bit. Less than 1% of all your youth, less than one sip from a glass."

"And we won't change at all?"

"Not at all really. You won't grow any smaller and you won't grow any bigger."

"Ha, ha," laughed the children, "who minds giving up a tiny bit of youth in exchange for much more fun?"

"How is it done?"

Jolly-Goodday put on a very wise expression and showed them drawings and data sheets.

"At noon, when the sun is at its highest, I'll take a big nail and nail the sun to the heavens above your island. Then it'll always be day and always be bright and you can fly and fly endlessly as much as you want without sleeping ever again."

"Wow! Fantastic!" said the children.

Everyone waited impatiently for noon. Then Jolly-Goodday got up out of his deck chair, went into his spaceship, and fetched a gigantic ladder, an enormous hammer, and a stupendous nail. He rested the ladder on the end of a white cloud.

Jolly-Goodday put on pitch-black sunglasses to avoid being blinded and slipped polka-dot oven mitts over his hands to avoid being sunburned. He then climbed with the hammer and nail high up into the blue sky and nailed the nail into the middle of the sun with a noise that echoed throughout the whole world.

BANG! BANG! BANG!

Golden sunbeams flew everywhere and landed in the sea hissing and bubbling. Jolly-Goodday then jumped off the ladder and glided down to earth in a flower-patterned parachute.

"The sun won't leave now, kids. You need never again say good morning or goodnight. Eternal day reigns on your island."

"Hooray, hooray," shouted the children, "now there's eternal day. Jolly-Goodday's got the answer to everything."

It's safe to say there had never been as much fun for the children on the island as right at that moment. The sun was always high in the sky and never moved, but shone and shone so that no one needed to sleep. The flowers blossomed with loud bangs and the island became a sea of flowers in the ocean. The lemons turned yellow. The apples reddened. The trees turned green and grew with cracks and groans, and the growing of the grass could be heard far out to sea.

The kids could fly and fly and no one noticed the passing of time.

Solar Utilization Standard Deviations

Fig. 1

Fig. 2

100%

Comparison of Peak Sunlight Hours

They saw no stars in the sky, just continuous noontime sunshine and endless fun and games, and no one was bored for a single minute. Everyone was ecstatically happy, with suntans, broad smiles, and tummies full of butterflies.

Wolf! Wolf!

But then the clouds covered the sun. First a small one, and then more and more came until the sky was full of clouds. Then came pouring rain. The children sat under trees in a foul mood.

"Oh, I hate rain," whined Elva.

"Me too," said Magni dejectedly.

"You don't get a belly full of butterflies in the rain," muttered Brimir.

The kids waded through the mud and slush on the beach to Jolly-Goodday's where he lay under the flower-patterned parachute, using it as an umbrella.

"It's really intolerable when you're innocently flying along and the clouds suddenly cover the sun. It's highly dangerous. You could simply crash to the ground and be smashed to pieces," said Hulda. She was quite furious.

"Yeah, that's right. We can't have rain getting out of control and taking everyone by surprise! Rain is boring!"

"Down with rain! Down with rain!"

Jolly-Goodday thought long and deeply.

"I think I can fix this, dear kids, and it shouldn't cost much."

The children brightened up.

"How?"

"Look at the clouds in the sky."

They all looked down at their feet.

"Look at the clouds, kids, don't be silly."

"But they're so unexciting, we can't be bothered to stare at them anymore," said Brimir. "We want to fly, that's exciting!"

"But what do the clouds look like?"

The children gawped listlessly up into the sky.

"Why don't you tell us instead? We don't want to look at clouds. We want to fly higher than the clouds."

"Shall I tell you what I think?" asked Jolly-Goodday. "I think the clouds look like little woolly lambs that have come here to pee on you," he said as he burst out laughing.

"Ugh, what disgusting lambs," said the children. "Just as well they don't poop on us too."

"But how does one get rid of these pesky lambs?" asked Jolly-Goodday.

"You scare them away," said Hulda grinning.

"And what are lambs scared of?"

"They're scared of the big bad wolf!" shouted Brimir.

"That's right!"

Jolly-Goodday took a large fat cigar from his back pocket and lighted it. He sucked and blew, sucked and blew, coughed and blew, and a horrid cloud of smoke came from his ears. His nose smoked like a factory

chimney. His mouth was like an exhaust pipe. The smoke rose up in the sky and gathered in a black and ominous cloud. The cloud grew bigger and bigger and became uglier and uglier. When the cigar was burned to ashes Jolly-Goodday looked proudly up into the sky.

"Well, how do you like it?"

"The ugly black cloud?" asked the children.

"How do you like the wolf!"

The children looked thunderstruck up into the sky and saw that the black cloud was just like a big, fierce wolf. Jolly-Goodday waved his arms and cried:

"Wolf! Wolf! Go get the lambs that pee rain on the kids!
Wolf! Wolf! Go get the lambs that throw shadows on them too!"

From the sky came the most terrifying growl they had ever heard. It was like a thousand thunderstorms, and from the wolf's eyes and mouth shot streaks of lightning. The wolf raced across the heavens and swallowed a few lamb-clouds in one big bite.

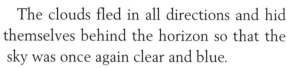

The clouds fled in all directions and hid themselves behind the horizon so that the sky was once again clear and blue.

After that not a single cloud was seen in the sky apart from the black one, which ran like a wolf round the horizon making sure that no cloud ever came over it.

"Hooray," shouted the children. "If Jolly-Goodday hadn't saved us we would have been bored to death in the rain."

"Is the wolf dangerous?" asked Hulda.

"Not unless you fly bleating like a lamb through the sky in a white woollen sweater."

"Could it swallow the sun?"

Jolly-Goodday made no answer.

"How . . . how much does the wolf cost?" asked Brimir.

"Oh, nothing at all really," said Jolly-Goodday, "maybe just a little more youth."

"You need more youth?"

"I need just a teeny-weeny drop more, hardly enough worth mentioning. Within 10% of usable youth."

"We don't really understand this % stuff."

"How do you collect youth?" asked Arnar the thinker.

"Are we really interested in listening to some boring vacuum-cleaner-techno-baloney?" asked Jolly-Goodday.

"You don't need to understand. Can't you see that the sun's shining and the sky is clear and blue?"

"Hooray," shouted the children and they flew off into the air.

They went higher and higher until they became little black dots in the clear blue sky. The whole island echoed with the shouts of children's laughter, which drowned even the noise of the screeching terns and wailing gulls. Sometimes a wondrous cry could be heard when they saw something new and amazing. Sometimes sighs of happiness could be heard when the children tasted delicious fruits that grew on the tallest trees, which they had never been able to reach before Jolly-Goodday had taught them to fly.

The scent of flowers filled the air. But soon a strange smell began to be borne on the wind. Wherever the children went they could smell the disgusting stink.

The Strangest Stink

"What is that stink, kids?" cried Jolly-Goodday from where he sat on the beach. He was lathered in suntan lotion and slurping a cold drink to keep himself cool.

"What stink?" asked the children innocently.

"It's not like the smell from a volcano, more like a mixture of rotten eggs and smelly feet," said Jolly-Goodday and grimaced. "Has someone just farted?"

The children looked all around.

"Oh, now I remember," said Magni, "it's farting season for the hippos."

"And the zebras air their toes at exactly this time of year," added Brimir.

"Are you trying to fool me, kids? It's impossible to breathe here."

Jolly-Goodday sprayed himself with an after-shave, which was so strong that flies dropped dead all around him.

There was a long silence.

"Actually we are fooling you," said Elva as she floated like a bee around a cherry tree in full bloom. "It's so boring to wash ourselves in the waterfall."

"The butterfly powder could be washed off," said the children, "so we've stopped having baths."

"Aren't you suffocated by the stink?" asked Jolly-Goodday, holding his nose.

"If we fly fast enough the wind blows the stink away," said Elva as she whizzed past.

"My dear kiddies, it's the easiest thing in the world to fix this stink."

"Do you know a way to do that as well?"

"I know the answer to everything," said Jolly-Goodday. "Follow me to the waterfall."

The children glided in the direction of Fairmost Falls, hovering over Jolly-Goodday like seagulls as he walked along the path to the waterfall, which fell with a tremendous roar into a canyon. The children were overwhelmed when they felt the power of the waterfall. The roar was so loud it was difficult to hear anyone speak. A huge rainbow formed as the sun shone through the waterfall's misty spray.

"Just look at how depressing this is, kids," shouted Jolly-Goodday, looking down into the immensely deep canyon.

"What?" shouted the children surprised.

"A whole waterfall going to waste, of no use to anyone."

"But it's beautiful," exclaimed Elva.

"It's a childish waste of time to stare at waterfalls. Now watch carefully."

Jolly-Goodday rolled up his sleeves and took out a hammer. He beat the rainbow in the canyon from all directions and battered it into the shape of a little ball. He stirred into it all the waterfall's misty spray and its loud roar, and created a brown gooey mess, which he then thrust into an aerosol can. Rainbowless, roarless, and mistless, the waterfall trickled feebly into the canyon like a runny nose.

"What have you done?" whispered the children, listening to the silence.

"I made a magic stuff out of the roar, the spray, and the rainbow, so you'll never need to wash yourselves again," said Jolly-Goodday, and he shook the aerosol can before spraying the stuff over the children.

"Magic stuff?"

"This is Teflon® wonder stuff, which makes you so slippery that dirt and mud can never stick to you."

"So we'll never stink again?"

"Not while you're coated with Teflon® wonder stuff."

"Will we ever need to bathe in the waterfall mist?"

"Try lying in the mud," said Jolly-Goodday.

The kids rolled around in the mud but the dirt fell off them immediately. The children took the most disgusting filth they could find, full of dog-poop, rotten bananas, dead flies, and tiger pee, and threw it at each other. It made no difference. The filth ran off them. Their hands, nails, and bottoms were spotlessly clean. They were so spick-and-span that there wasn't even a whiff of smelly toes about them anymore.

"Thanks to the great Teflon® wonder stuff, you are so slippery that you can't even hold hands or hug each other," said Jolly-Goodday with a big smile. His teeth were as white and straight as a row of sugar cubes.

The children tried to hold hands but couldn't get a grip, they were more slippery than salmon, slimier than eels. They tried to hug each other, but no matter how hard they squeezed each other, no one could hold onto anyone. The kids burst out laughing, however, because they could still fly: the butterfly powder was under the magic stuff of course!

"Wow, you're not only the funniest man in the world but also by far the cleverest," said Brimir.

"How much does the Teflon® wonder stuff cost?"

"Oof, not much, just a small dash of youth in addition."

"Just a few %?" asked the children.

"Yes, just a very few % in addition."

The children realized it wasn't really expensive to pay with a little youth from the enormously deep well in order to do without having to bathe themselves in the cold waterfall spray.

"Hooray for Jolly-Goodday!"

Now everything was really perfect for the children on

the island and they danced in the blue sky. They could fly whenever they wanted, the sun shone all day, the sky was clear and blue, and they were coated with Teflon® wonder stuff, which kept them squeaky clean.

"And now you're ready for the flying competition of the century!" cried Jolly-Goodday. "More speed! More excitement! More fun!"

"Hooray," shouted the children. "Now we're really going to have a good time!"

The Great Flying Competition and into the Blue

Jolly-Goodday took a loudspeaker and blared out:

"The great flying competition is about to begin. Now we'll really find out who's the best on the island!"

The children looked at Jolly-Goodday in amazement.

"But everyone's the best at something."

"But the one who's the best at flying is the very best of all, and now it's time for the flying fun competition!"

"I pick Hulda," said Brimir.

"No, no, there's no fun having people in teams," said Jolly-Goodday. "Let's have everyone against everyone else instead. The one who reaches the highest is the best of you all. Off you go!"

The kids shot up into the air shouting and screaming. Elva and Magni were equal in first place and zoomed like jet fighters straight up into the sky, but a black and white flock of terns jabbed them back down to the ground. Arnar the thinker then took the lead, but he collided with a gaggle of geese and crashed to the ground with them. Brimir and Hulda were soon, by far and away, flying the highest.

"I must get above her," thought Brimir, and with difficulty climbed just a fraction higher than Hulda.

They were now the only ones left in the competition and were soaring at a fearful height. The land below seemed tiny and the children on the ground were no longer even little dots, indeed the lakes and forests were like little blue and green spots.

They had reached higher than the jabbing terns, higher than the gliding gannets, higher than the soaring swans, and finally even higher than the eager eagle. They had reached as high as the butterfly powder would allow them and they would have been dead level if Brimir's hair hadn't stood on end.

"Ha, ha! Tough luck! I win! You lose!" called out Brimir triumphantly.

Hulda's cheeks burned red. "Hair doesn't count."

"Ha, ha! Sure it does. Sour grapes!"

"I wished I could get much higher than you," shouted Hulda.

But Hulda had forgotten that she had an amazingly beautiful wishing stone. As soon as she had spoken the stone changed into an ordinary gray pebble and Hulda shot far up into the sky. Brimir managed to grab hold of her belt as they zoomed even higher at a tremendous speed.

"Cheater! I won, I'm the best!" cried Brimir.

"No, let me go! I won!"

Brimir bit Hulda's foot hard and she tore out a large chunk of his hair. And that's how they fought in the sky, propelled by the power of the wishing stone, higher and higher.

"Traitor!" shouted Brimir. "You destroyed the wishing stone."

"Idiot! I could make any wish I wanted."

Brimir and Hulda were now dangerously high in the sky. If a gust of wind hadn't blown them sideways they would certainly have flown far out into space and been lost, or made a hole in the ozone layer and been burned by the sun. The gust of wind blew them a very long way. They were blown over the high mountains and the narrow gorges, and finally far out to sea. But Brimir and Hulda did not see any of this because they were quarreling and squabbling, screaming and scratching, punching and pummelling. It was not until much later that they looked down and noticed that they couldn't see the island anymore. Below them was nothing but an endless ocean with whales and sharks, and in the distance a glint of unknown mountains, valleys, and clouds.

"Now see what you've done," cried Brimir. "We've been blown off into the blue."

"Blue? Where is this blue anyhow?"

"Oh, shut up, Hulda!"

"Oh, shut up yourself, Brimir, you jerk," said Hulda. "You just had to go and grab me."

"And I had to go and give you the wishing stone."

The children became silent as they were blown even further along. They were blown so far from the nailed sun that it became a red spot above the ocean in the west.

"Look!" said Brimir suddenly.

"What," said Hulda irritably.

"The sun is setting."

"So what."

"I'd forgotten how beautiful the sunset is," said Brimir.

Hulda said nothing, but Brimir noticed how she watched the sun set, how it was reflected in her eyes. The power of the butterfly powder only works in sunlight, however, and they had now been blown over to the other side of the planet. It was pitch-black there because the sun could only shine on one side of the planet at a time. Underneath the darkness lay a land with forests and lakes.

"Oh, no! We're falling!" shouted Brimir.

"Oh, I don't want to die," wailed Hulda.

They were falling fast. The wind whistled through their hair. The land approached with growing speed. They were now lower than the eager eagle, lower than the soaring swans, lower than the gliding gannets. They were now so low that they landed on the ground with a crash.

Wind-cold Wolf-trees

In a dark forest a weak sound could be heard from under the bushes.

"Hulda! Hulda! Are you all right?" Brimir felt his way with his hands. "Hulda, where are you?"

"I'm here, Brimir."

Her voice echoed in the gloom. When his eyes had gotten used to the darkness he could see where Hulda was hanging from a tree.

"Shall I help you down?" asked Brimir.

"I can manage by myself. Leave me alone!"

A great cracking sound could be heard as Hulda tumbled from the tree. Brimir hovered anxiously over her.

"Are you okay?"

"Leave me alone. It was the easiest way to get down."

Brimir was silent, but he saw that Hulda had hurt herself. They were in a forest, but the trees were bare and leafless. The wind whistled through the naked branches. The sky was full of clouds.

"What shall we do?" asked Brimir. "We're lost."

"We? Are you going to follow me? I don't need you."

Brimir remained silent and looked sadly at Hulda.

"But we'll never find our way in this darkness," he finally said.

"I'm going to wait until morning," said Hulda. "I can fly home when the sun comes up."

Hulda sat down under a tree and covered herself with a pile of faded leaves. Brimir walked dejectedly to another tree, rubbed together two sticks and lit a little fire with some dry twigs. In the fire's glow he saw Hulda shivering with cold.

"Don't you want to warm yourself by my fire, Hulda?"

She made no reply.

And that's how they sat waiting for daybreak. Hulda shivered and Brimir sat by the fire. The night was unbelievably long. Brimir was starving but no fruit could be found on the trees and there were no animals in sight. Exhausted, he fell asleep.

When Brimir woke up the sun had still not risen. Nonetheless he felt as if he'd slept long and well. After pondering this for a short while, his face suddenly turned deathly pale.

"Hulda!"

"What now, you jerk!"

"I don't think the sun's going to rise."

"Talk about being pessimistic! Of course the sun will rise."

"Haven't you forgotten something, Hulda? We let Jolly-Goodday fix the sun over our island so there'd be everlasting day."

"Oh, no," said Hulda. "And now we're on the other side of the planet in endless night."

"Which means we'll have to walk all the way home."

"Don't you think Jolly-Goodday will save us? He always saves the day and the kids must be getting worried about us."

Brimir and Hulda waited a while longer; they fell asleep and woke up a few times, but it was always to the same darkness and no one came to save them. Their tummies began to rumble in unison.

"They've forgotten us."

"Maybe they've forgotten you, but not me," said Hulda sulkily.

"But it's always noon on our island, they don't realize how long we've been missing."

"They must be on the way. I'm going to wait."

"I want to leave right now," said Brimir.

"Go then! See if I care."

Brimir set off into the forest. Hulda remained seated on her own.

"Wait a minute, Brimir!"

"Are you coming with me?"

"No, I'm going to walk behind you, so the wild animals will eat you first."

Brimir didn't answer her, but Hulda followed right behind him. They got stung by thistles and stumbled over fallen tree trunks.

In the darkness the trees were like ogres and monsters; their branches were long gnarled hands that stretched out to catch them and keep them in the forest. Sometimes they creaked and cracked as if they could talk:

*Creak and crack, crimping Brimir, branches blasted
  and broke,*
*Bleak and black, mangling Brimir, crack, crunch,
  and croak.*

"Oh," said Brimir, "this is like my worst nightmare."
Sometimes the whining of the wind in the trees was like a ghostly groan from the forest.

Wh-o-o hiss Huuuldaaaa, who-o-m we'll h-o-old,
Here in the eerie, ho-o-owling co-o-old!
We-e'll haunt and taunt her, a-a-ll al-o-o-one,
We'll h-o-o-ld and h-i-i-ide her, fa-a-r from h-o-ome!

"Brimir!"
It was Hulda who shouted.
Brimir came to a halt. "What?"
"There's one thing we should do before we go any further," said Hulda.

"What's that?" asked Brimir brusquely.

"We should try and be friends again, otherwise we'll never get home."

Brimir tried to look at Hulda but could see nothing in the dark. Nothing except a little tear, which glistened in her eye.

"Yeah, you're my dearest buddy, let's be friends again," said Brimir.

"Oh, Brimir, and you're my very best friend. Forgive me for being so nasty to you."

Brimir tried to give Hulda a hug but couldn't; they were so slippery from the Teflon® wonder stuff.

The children crept on through the forest. They were still shivering from fear and cold, and their tummies rumbled from hunger, but their hearts were warm with friendship once more.

They hadn't gone very far when they heard a ferocious growl behind them. Brimir turned around and looked straight into the jaws of a large brown bear. Its teeth were as sharp as icicles.

The Fierce Grizzly

Brimir and Hulda were frozen with fear as the bear stood on its hind legs and roared. They could not move an arm or leg. At last Hulda managed to stammer:

"Please don't eat us, Grizzly, we're innocent little children."

The bear growled in reply. "I haven't had a bite to eat since the sun disappeared and now I'm going to gobble up every last bit of you."

"Oh, no! Brimir! This is our last moment!"

The children closed their eyes as the bear sniffed their bellies and snorted.

"Huh, huh," he growled a little, sniffed again, and then roared. "You're not children. What are you?"

"Wh . . . what do you mean?" asked Brimir.

"You're not even humans," said the bear pulling a face. "You're something horribly inedible."

Hulda's face was burning red.

"What do you mean, horribly inedible?" she demanded.

"You don't smell like children, you just have a faint scent of butterfly. You're either plastic children or zombies," said the bear as he looked around fearfully. His fur stood on end when he mentioned zombies.

Brimir gave Hulda a nudge, but she took no notice.

"We're not plastic and we're not zombies, we're real live children," shouted Hulda, who was now quite furious.

The bear then roared:

"No, you're not. I know the scent of delicious child flesh, and you're not butterflies either, because they're in all the colors of the rainbow and fly after the sun once a year. That's when all the bears fall in love and make cubs, because the flight of the butterflies is the most beautiful thing in the world."

The bear turned around sadly and disappeared in the forest.

"We are children, we can prove it," shouted Hulda furiously at the bear.

"Cut it out, Hulda! What are you trying to do, get the bear to eat us?"

"WE ARE REAL CHILDREN! WE ARE REAL CHILDREN!" shouted Hulda into the darkness.

"We are real children! We are real children!" replied the darkness.

Hulda sat down on a rock and began to cry.

"Don't cry, Hulda. We got away from the bear alive."

"No, we're dead, we died when we fell from the sky."

"Don't be silly, we're alive and kicking," said Brimir reassuringly, but he tried to feel for his heartbeat just to be sure.

"Didn't you hear what the bear said? He said that we weren't children, but zombies, and that's why he wouldn't eat us. Have you ever heard of a bear that didn't eat children?"

"Hulda, don't you understand? We got away because we've got the butterfly powder on our hands and we're coated with Teflon® wonder stuff, which makes us so spick-and-span that we don't have any smell, just a faint scent of butterflies."

Hulda wiped the tears from her eyelids.

"So Jolly-Goodday's saved our lives by coating us with stuff that makes bears lose their appetite?"

"See," said Brimir. "Jolly-Goodday always saves the day."

The children continued walking through the dark forest with the naked branches. They hadn't gone very far when they heard the echo again:

"We are real children! We are real children! **Ha ha ha ha ha!!!**"

"That was a very late echo," said Brimir.

"It wasn't an echo," said Hulda, and listened more attentively.

The sound came from every direction and was approaching them.

Hairy Spiders and Poisonous Insects

"We are real children! We are real children! Ha ha ha ha!!!!"

Brimir and Hulda listened intently.

"Who's playing copycat?" Hulda cried out into the dark.

"Who's playing copycat? Who's playing copycat? Who's playing copycat?" answered the darkness.

The children stared into the dark forest between the tree trunks and the distant sound of a song reached their ears:

Eightlegs, Bluebottlecruncher,
Tanglepegs, Caterpillarmuncher,
Go spin, yes, go spin.
Weaverbug and Spinningtop,
Uglyjug and Slobberchop,
Go spin, yes, go spin,
With evil intent.
Go smell, yes, go smell,
The butterfly scent.

"Look at the web," said Brimir pointing at a large spider's web stretched between the tree branches.

"And over there too," said Hulda.

"And up there above us as well!"

Let's listen, let's listen,
To the children prate.
Let's weave, let's weave
Them a web of fate.

A hairy spider spun itself down from the highest tree and hung on a thread directly in front of them.

"Hello, meal, my name's Eightlegs and I'm going to eat you."

Brimir remembered what the bear had said and hurriedly exclaimed:

"We're no meal, we're horribly inedible. Can't you smell the butterfly scent?"

"Oh, we most certainly can smell the butterfly scent," shrieked Eightlegs. "Butterflies are a feast!"

"Hush Brimir," whispered Hulda. "We're children. Spiders eat butterflies, not children."

"That's right, Eightlegs, a silly slip of the tongue," said Brimir. "We're children, and spiders don't eat children."

The spider burst out laughing. "Ha ha ha ha!"

Brimir wanted to continue their journey and blurted out, "Go away you ugly spider, you can't eat children, so stop trying to scare us."

The spider waved its legs in gleeful anticipation.

"Once upon a time we ate only flies and bugs and weaved our webs at night. But now it's always dark so we can weave even bigger webs and eat birds and squirrels and sometimes monkeys. Life has never been better and we've never been fatter. Ho ho ho."

"One small spider can't eat a child," said Brimir.

"But a million spiders will have no problem!" said Eightlegs and laughed.

More laughter reached them from the darkness like a choir of a million voices. They looked up at the treetops and saw thousands of spiders with hairy legs spinning their way down towards them.

Let's spin, yes, let's spin,
With evil intent.
Let's smell, yes, let's smell,
The butterfly scent.

"Run for it!" shouted Brimir, and off they fled.

Let's weave, yes, let's weave
To trap and deceive.
Then sip and sup on blood,
Sip and sup on children's blood.

"Don't touch the spider's web," cried Hulda, "you'll never get out of it."

"No web in that direction," shouted Brimir, and they ran on again.

The children ran and ran and were so busy looking all around them they failed to notice the web right in front of them. It was for certain the largest web ever woven in the forest, and they were heading straight for it.

The Butterfly Monsters

"Brimir! Did you see what happened?"

"Are we stuck in the web?" asked Brimir, opening his eyes carefully.

He looked round and saw shreds of the web hanging in the trees and a spider choir of a million voices yelling after them:

"We'll get you sooner or later!"

"Jolly-Goodday saved us once again!" shouted Brimir.

"How come?"

"Because we're coated with Teflon® wonder stuff from the waterfall's roar, misty spray, and rainbow, we're so slippery that nothing can stick to us, not even the largest and stickiest spider's web in the world."

"Hooray for Jolly-Goodday who thinks of everything!"

"Let's hurry on home and thank him."

"It'll be great to get home to all the fun and the sun and the craze for flying."

Brimir and Hulda continued their journey through dark forests and over gloomy plains in search of their island so bright and joyful. They crossed frozen lakes and deep valleys and back into forests again and over plains.

They sometimes munched on nuts or dug up potatoes, but most often they walked for hours without getting anything to appease their hunger. Occasionally they crossed the path of a lion or a tiger, but the animals of the forest had no appetite for children who didn't smell of soft meat and warm blood.

The animals sniffed them.

"You're not human, you smell like a butterfly," said the tiger who was going to gobble up Brimir.

"You're not human, you're as smooth as steel," said the python who tried to crush Hulda.

Brimir and Hulda had ceased to be afraid of wild animals. Indeed, the wild animals were now afraid of them, the horribly inedible children, and stories about them spread through the forest. The wild animals called them the butterfly monsters. Brimir and Hulda enjoyed walking calmly past a pack of wolves and catching the glint of fear in the wild animals' eyes. They slept fearlessly in a bear's lair or crept up on lions simply to startle them.

The children came to a glade where a large and fierce leopard was about to eat a sheep. Hulda crept up behind the leopard, which caught no scent of a child and so concentrated on the sheep. Hulda came right up to it, holding in her laughter, before she yelled and pulled the leopard's tail:

"Boo! Boo! I'm the butterfly monster! I'm going to eat you!"

The leopard howled pitifully and rushed away while Brimir and Hulda held their sides laughing. They rubbed their empty tummies before eating up every last bit of the lamb.

Replenished, they continued their journey. The sky was always clouded over so that they couldn't follow the moon or find their way by the stars. Sometimes they thought they saw a shining star, but it was only a firefly with its deceptive glowing light. The cries of night owls and bats pierced the darkness, but otherwise the night was songless. The birds had flown away in search of the sun. Abandoned chicks cheeped in their nests.

The children had been walking for a long time but had no idea for how long exactly because they measured time in days, and the sun no longer circled the planet.

It began to pour with rain. A thousand woolly and curly lambs in the sky peed over the children. They found shelter in a large cave and lit a little yellow fire with dried leaves.

"We'll never find our way home," said Brimir sadly, "and I'm hungry again."

"We'll find no food in this downpour."

They became silent and sat staring at the fire when

Hulda had an idea. She walked grinning to the cave mouth and shouted out into the darkness:

"Lion! We want meat, right now!"

"Why should I give you meat?" growled the lion in the darkness.

"Should we eat you instead?" growled Hulda, and she bared her teeth. "You don't know what a butterfly monster can do in a fit of rage."

The lion appeared shortly after with a little reindeer in its jaws.

"That wasn't so difficult," said Hulda, and smiled.

"Some vegetables would be nice," said Brimir.

"Mole! Bring some potatoes!" yelled Hulda.

"What if I don't feel like it?" was heard muttered from beneath the forest.

"Then we'll eat you," said Hulda, stamping her foot.

A pile of potatoes came up through the cave floor.

"I'm still hungry," said Brimir when they had finished the reindeer and potatoes.

"Call for food. There's a delivery service in this forest."

"Mink! We'd like some fish!" shouted Brimir.

"I've trouble enough fending for myself," replied the mink in the darkness.

"I've never tasted mink meat before!" cried Brimir, and he tried to growl like Hulda.

Soon afterwards a fat and wriggling trout appeared at the mouth of the cave.

"I'm thirsty," sighed Brimir after his meal. "I'd like some milk."

"She-wolf, we want some milk."

The she-wolf came and lay down by the children. They snuggled up to her warm pelt and sucked warm wolf-milk from her teats. Their sleep was passed in wolf dreams: Yellow moon. Black darkness. Red blood.

The Wildest Wild Animals

When Hulda and Brimir awoke the she-wolf had gone and the fire was cold. The darkness was so dense one could almost feel it.

"Bears! Firewood!" yelled the children.

Bears flocked to the cave, each with an armful of sticks and logs. They built a large bonfire, which Brimir set alight. The fire burned like a little sun and shone out through the cave entrance.

"Maybe it's possible to fly in the glow of the fire if the flames are powerful enough," said Hulda staring at the bonfire.

Brimir's eyes gleamed. "Bears! More firewood!" he shouted.

The bears added a whole tree to the pile. The fire blazed more and more intensely.

Until at last . . .

"I can fly!" cried Hulda. "HA! HA! HA!"

The children glided like flies around the bonfire, wildly ecstatic. Circleaftercircleaftercircle. The flames licked the

roof of the cave. The rain pounded down outside. Lightning lit up the forest. Shrieking bats joined them.

"We are wolf-cubs! We are black hornets! Everyone's afraid of us! We're the wildest of wild animals!"

The dark shadows flickered.

"Spiders and silkworms! We need clothing!"

"Why should we spin and weave for you?"

"Because otherwise we'll rip down your webs! We are the butterfly monsters, the strongest and most ferocious of wild animals. You have to obey us!"

The worms span their finest silk, and the spiders wove from it precious clothes in thousands of colors. The children put reindeer horns on their heads and flew screaming around the flames.

"We don't have to hurry home. We're fine right here!"

"Hyena! We're hungry!"

The hyena laughed its cynical laugh and set off into the forest. Shortly afterwards it came with its prey in its jaws and laid it on the cave floor. The children looked horrified at its catch.

"It's a child!"

The child lay motionless on the cave floor, its face deathly pale. It was a boy about the same size as Brimir.

"Is he dead?" whispered Hulda.

"Hee, hee, hee," shrieked the hyena. "I thought you'd want fresh meat and would kill him yourself. Aren't you the wildest of wild animals? Hee, hee, hee!"

The hyena ran away laughing.

Brimir ran up to the child and began to revive him.

"Is he hurt?"

"I don't see any blood."

"What's a child doing wandering around in such a dark and dangerous forest?" asked an outraged Hulda.

Brimir looked at her.

"The forest wasn't always so black. Before we fixed the sun over our island at home it had been almost certainly just like our forest, light green and dark green in turns, depending on the sunshine and moonlight."

Brimir gave the boy some wolf-milk to drink. He soon came round, but his face remained amazingly pale.

"Who are you?" he asked, wide-eyed.

"We're Brimir and Hulda."

"Did the hyena eat you too?"

"No, we rescued you from it," said Brimir.

The boy stood up and dusted off the soil and animal slobber.

"My name's Darrow. Thanks for saving my life, but now I have to hurry back to my friends. They think I'm dead."

"Are there more children in the forest?"

"Well over a hundred. They tried to save me, but the hyena was so fierce."

"How will you get home? It's impossible to find your way in the dark."

"I know a way," said Darrow.

Darrow went outside the cave and caught some luminous fireflies, which swam like radiant fish in the dark.

"It's like he's collecting stars from heaven," whispered Hulda.

Darrow took the fireflies to the nearest oak tree and dipped them in the sticky tree sap. He then stuck them onto his forehead where they cast a pale blue glow into the forest. Brimir and Hulda followed right behind him.

"This way, my friends are over there," said Darrow, when a glow could be seen in the distance.

The flies on his forehead buzzed and lit up the way. His eyes looked strange in this light. His teeth bluish. His skin greeny-blue. When they came over a low hill they saw the glow came from a jar full of thousands of buzzing fireflies, shining like a full moon. Round the jar sat creatures warbling weird songs.

"Are you sure Darrow's alive?" whispered Hulda. "He's so ghostly."

Darrow came to a halt and looked round slowly. The firefly light was so strong they had to squint.

"Come Brimir. Come Hulda. Come and meet my friends."

"If Darrow's dead, then his friends are zombies and ghost children," whispered Hulda, a tingle of fear running down her spine.

The Ghost Children

"Come," said Darrow, trying to pull them along.

The ghostly children sang beautiful songs about the sun and the butterflies. They sang about sunrise and sunset, birds and flowers, and fruits and a sky that was sometimes blue or white and sometimes red or full of glittering stars. They sang with sorrow about Darrow who had ended up in the belly of a fierce hyena.

"Stop singing that, I'm here," shouted Darrow.

The song ceased. The creatures by the firefly-light looked round.

"It's Darrow," they cried. "Darrow's alive! Darrow's alive!"

The children rushed round Darrow and hugged him. There were certainly well over a hundred of them.

"Oh, Darrow, our dearest best friend, we cried so much," said a little girl with black eyes.

Brimir looked at Hulda and tears came into his eyes. "That's how glad to see us everyone will be if we ever get home."

Darrow had been kissed so much he needed to wipe his face. "This is Brimir and this is Hulda," he said. "They saved me."

"Weren't you scared of the hyena and the predators in the forest?"

Brimir was going to explain everything. "No, you see, we're coated with TEF…"

But Hulda interrupted him. "Yes, we were dreadfully scared."

"Where do you come from?" asked the children.

"We come from an island in the big ocean on the other side of the planet, and my name is Brimir."

"Hooray for Brimir the Brave!"

"And I'm Hulda."

"Hooray for Hulda the Heroine!"

"Are you looking for the sun?" asked a thin boy.

"Have you seen it?" asked Brimir, brightening up.

"A very long time ago. One evening the sun set, as it's done every day for a million years, and then no one knows what became of it."

"Our forest is dying and the birds have flown away and we sit here in the cold singing odes to the sun and sharing our last bite to eat. We will soon die from hunger."

Brimir looked at Hulda. When Jolly-Goodday fixed the sun over their island they had forgotten about the children on the other side of the planet.

"At first we found it very beautiful because we always had the moon and stars, but then the clouds started to pile up. Since then the sky has either been pitch-black or dark gray and we've sat here by the fire thinking about the butterflies that can only fly in sunlight. But there's never any sun here."

Hulda and Brimir hung their heads dejectedly. When the wolf chased the clouds out of the sky over their island, he had driven them all here.

"Is it also dark and cold on the other side of the planet where you live?" asked a little girl with blond hair.

Brimir paled. He felt his legs trembling and was heavy at heart. There was a long silence until he muttered:

"No, we haven't seen the sun, there's no sun in our country. Hulda and I were sent on an expedition to find it."

As soon as he said this he felt a terrible pang of remorse in his heart.

"Yes, what Brimir says is true. It's actually colder on our island and the darkness even blacker, a really dreadful situation," said Hulda, who also felt an awful pang of remorse.

"And that's why the butterflies can't fly anymore," said Brimir. And felt an even greater pang in his heart.

"I'm sorry to hear that," said a girl. "But why are your faces so brown?"

"Th-th-th-that's because we eat so much soil to keep alive, all the food on our island is finished," stammered Brimir, biting his lower lip.

"Everything's so ugly and horrible when the sun doesn't shine."

The pale children listened sadly to Brimir and Hulda's story.

"You're really having a hard time," said a boy, "because in spite of the dark and the cold there are still many beautiful things around us."

"The ice on the lake is sometimes as smooth as a mirror, and sometimes wrinkled in waves, and at other times it can be all broken up, like a mound of scrap metal. It's scary, but beautiful all the same."

"We also know some beautiful poems about butter-flies."

"And we can tell stories about the sun."

But then the children's faces became sad.

"Stories of the sun can't bring the forest back to life, though. If the forest dies, we die too."

"And the butterflies don't fly here, in spite of the poems."

"But we can hug each other when we feel really down."

There was a long silence until Darrow whispered something to a child who whispered it to the next child. At last all the pale children disappeared into the depths of the forest one by one. Brimir and Hulda sat silently with an aching heart and soul.

"Why did we say the darkness was blacker and the hunger worse back home?" asked Brimir sadly.

"They'd have been furious if they knew we'd got Jolly-Goodday to fix the sun over our island and to make a wolf-cloud that drives the annoying clouds over to their sky."

"And if they only knew what we did with the butterfly powder."

They sat listening to the fireflies buzzing in the jar when they heard some movement from out of the darkness. The children with the pale faces had returned. Darrow was at their head and dragged a huge sack behind him.

The pale children appeared from every direction.

"Do you think they heard what we said?" whispered Brimir.

They were just about to run away when Darrow spoke.

"Ever since the sun disappeared we've been sewing this air balloon together so that we can go and look for it. But now we know there's darkness on the other side of the planet too, you may as well use the balloon to get back home."

Darrow came over to Hulda and Brimir and kissed them on the cheek.

"Thank you for saving my life."

Hulda was taken aback and looked mournfully at Brimir.

"We can't take your air balloon. We'll manage on our own," said Brimir.

The pale children were still determined to help them,

nonetheless. They filled the balloon with warm air and it slowly rose from the ground.

"Here are two pieces of bread and five pieces of dried fish to take with you," said Darrow and he handed Brimir a little basket.

"Get aboard quickly! The balloon is rising!"

"You'll never in your life have flown so high before!"

Brimir and Hulda remained motionless, but it was useless for them to resist. They were literally thrown into the basket. The air balloon glided up over the black forest and the pale children waved goodbye.

"Have a good trip home, you guys. And don't be scared of heights!"

The pale children became smaller and smaller the higher they floated. All that could be seen was a very dull glow where the firefly-light illuminated the forest. At last even that disappeared into total darkness.

Brimir and Hulda sat silently in the basket under the balloon. "Thank you for saving my life," Darrow had said. If he only knew who'd sent the hyena to hunt for food. "Don't be scared of heights," the pale children had said. If they only knew how high they had been under the nailed sun. The air balloon drifted across the sky in the pitch-black darkness. Not a sound could be heard except the whine of the wind as it blew through the ropes holding the basket.

"I feel ill at heart," whispered Hulda.

"I think there's a hole in my soul," said Brimir.

"We shouldn't have lied to the pale children."

The balloon floated on. The children slept. Brimir woke up to a mysterious sound.

"Listen," whispered Brimir.

They listened hopefully to the song that carried through the night.

"Is it a bird?" whispered Brimir.

"It's a night raven," said Hulda sadly. "It's a long way to the sun."

The children didn't know for how long or in what direction the balloon was carried. They tried to keep time by counting their heartbeats but they could only count up to a hundred. When they had counted up to a hundred a hundred times they had to stop. They knew that the air balloon must sooner or later be borne to their beautiful island. Sometimes the balloon was blown through clouds, which felt as if a cold fog enveloped them. Once the balloon rose up above the thick clouds and they floated for a short time under the moon and stars. They could see each other's faces in the golden glow of the moon. Brimir stroked Hulda's hair.

"Your hair's turned gray," said Brimir and looked closer. "You look old."

"Isn't that just the moonlight? You look gray-haired too."

"No, your hair's totally gray," said Brimir.

Hulda stared at Brimir's hair and saw that he was right. They had both become gray-haired.

"It's probably because of the darkness of the forest," said Hulda. "I hope it'll get better in the sunlight back home."

"If we get home," said Brimir, very depressed.

Below them lay a thick bank of clouds that spread out like white lava or a glacier full of cracks. When the balloon sank beneath the clouds again everything was black once more.

Sometimes they could hear birdsong.

"Is that a redwing?" asked Brimir hopefully

"No, it's a nightingale. It's still a long way to the sun."

They heard all kinds of night-bird sounds and the shriek of bats, but they never heard the sounds of birds that sing in the sun.

"Maybe we'll never find the sun," said Brimir.

"Maybe we'll die of hunger and end up as gray-haired skeletons in a floating air balloon."

"And the person who finds us will never sleep again without having nightmares," said Brimir sadly.

"If we get back home alive, we must help the children in the darkness and send them the sun before it's too late."

"And let the butterflies fly around the planet like they did in the old days," said Brimir.

The basket under the balloon rocked them to sleep. A chilly wind blew and the children tried to huddle closer together.

Ha ha ha ha ha ha.

Brimir and Hulda woke up to a familiar sound.

"Cuck—oo! Cuck—oo!"

"Yet another nightingale?" muttered Brimir tiredly.

Hulda peeked over the edge of the basket.

"No! Listen, it's a cuckoo! And there's daylight on the horizon!"

"It's the sun!" shouted Brimir. "And our island is under the sun!"

The island rose out of the sea like a green whale. The yellow sun shone brightly with the nail in its center, and the clouds became fewer and fewer until there was nothing above them but a clear blue. A heavenly bird-song could be heard from the island, a delight to their ears, but far away in the distance the black wolf-cloud drifted like a pirate ship.

"We're home at last!"

"I'm even glad to see the ugly wolf-cloud," said Brimir, smiling.

He had hardly let the words out of his mouth when thunder crashed and lightning flashed and the wolf-cloud speedily set off.

"Now the wolf's going to chase away clouds," said Brimir. He looked around excitedly, but couldn't see so much as a single wisp of cloud.

"What cloud is the wolf going to swallow, anyway?"

Brimir looked carefully at the balloon that was carrying them. He nudged Hulda.

"Doesn't the balloon remind you of anything?"

"Just seems like an ordinary balloon to me."

"Can't you see it's made of wool? It's as woolly as a lamb!"

Lightning flashed. Thunder boomed. The black wolf-cloud approached the air balloon with wide-open jaws.

"Quick! Jump!" shouted Brimir.

They jumped out of the air balloon just before the wolf swallowed it in one bite. The children were in free-fall while they remained in the wolf's shadow. He was quick to rush away in search of other clouds, however, and then the sun shone on the children and the butterfly powder on their hands. They could fly again!

"We'll survive, thanks to the butterfly powder!"

"Thanks to Jolly-Goodday!"

Brimir and Hulda glided over the land. It was more beautiful than ever before. The yellow waves of sand in the desert could hardly be seen for the buttercups swaying in the breeze. The trees had grown twice as large and birds sang on every branch. The children gobbled up colorful fruits that fell from the trees. Little black dots shot around in the air like flies.

Ha ha ha *ha* **ha** ha ha ha ha
ha **ha** ha ha
ha ha ha
ha **ha**
Ha ha ha **ha** ha ha
ha ha *ha* **ha** ha **ha** ha
ha ha ha ha ha
ha
ha *ha ha* **ha** ha ha **ha** ha *ha* **ha**

"Can you hear the laughter, Brimir? Everyone's so happy to see us safe and sound."

"We're home!"

Their friends rushed backward and forward and up and down. But no one came to welcome Brimir and Hulda.

"Aren't they laughing because we're safe and sound?" asked Hulda, looking around in amazement.

No one seemed to take any notice of them and they had no need to wipe wet kisses off their faces. Brimir tried to grab hold of Elva, but it was like trying to grab a car on the highway.

"I'm busy. There's so much fun right now. Ha ha ha ha ha ha. Must fly. Bye. Ha ha ha ha ha."

"Weren't you looking for us? We were lost in a dark forest."

"Lost? Who's lost?"

"We were lost," shouted Brimir. "Weren't you even worried about us? We could have died."

"Worried? Ha ha ha ha ha. We don't have to worry about anything. Jolly-Goodday tells such funny jokes. Whenever we have thoughts or worries on our minds they are changed immediately into jokes and we start laughing, ha ha ha ha. We stop thinking and forget about everything except the jokes."

A great noise of laughter and merriment could be heard from down on Black Beach. Jolly-Goodday stood there in red shorts, calling out through a huge loud-speaker.

"What's green, lives a yard underground, and eats stones?"

"What?" replied the children.

"A green stone-eater!"

The children laughed and laughed so much their laughter resounded through the mountains.

ha ha ha ha ha ha ha ha ha ha ha ha ha ha ha ha ha
ha ha ha ha ha ha ha ha ha ha ha ha ha ha ha ha ha
ha ha ha ha ha ha ha ha ha ha ha ha ha ha ha ha ha
ha ha ha ha ha ha ha ha ha ha ha ha ha ha ha ha ha
ha ha ha ha ha ha ha ha ha ha ha ha ha ha ha ha ha
ha ha ha ha ha ha ha ha ha ha ha ha ha ha ha ha ha
ha ha ha ha ha ha ha ha ha ha ha ha ha ha ha ha ha
ha ha ha ha ha ha ha ha ha ha ha ha ha ha ha ha ha
ha ha ha ha ha ha ha ha ha ha ha ha ha ha ha ha ha

Brimir and Hulda were a little bewildered.

"Everybody's so busy flying and listening to jokes that no one even noticed we were missing," said Brimir.

"But they're certainly having a lot of fun," said Hulda. It was quite a funny joke.

"Shouldn't we tell them about the pale children in the darkness?"

"If the nail is removed from the sun and the butterfly powder returned, we'll never ever fly again."

"Shall we use this last chance to fly?" asked Brimir.

"We must try to rest and recover a little after all the darkness, and get rid of our gray hair."

Hulda took off into the air and Brimir was going to follow her when he felt a pang of remorse in his heart once more. The same pang as when they met the children in the darkness and told them they didn't know where the sun was.

"Hulda, come on down to earth. I feel so bad."

"What's wrong?"

"I feel as if a little bug's gnawing at my soul. I can't forget the pale children in the darkness," said Brimir.

"Me neither."

"How can we help them?"

"Let's talk to Jolly-Goodday, he always saves the day."

"We also have to thank him for saving our lives."

Jolly-Goodday the Comedian

Brimir and Hulda flew low to the ground down to Black Beach where they met Jolly-Goodday. He sat in the sand building sandcastles. By his side lay the loudspeaker. He smiled when they arrived.

"Well, hello there, Brimir, and you too, Hulda! Aren't you in a good mood? Shall I tell you a joke? My goodness you do look smart."

"What do you mean, smart?" asked Brimir, forgetting to correct his name.

"You're so silver gray-haired, and she's more stoney-gray, very smart."

"You think it's cool for a child to have gray hair?"

"Do I think it's cool? Gray's in fashion. Where have you been?" asked Jolly-Goodday, shocked.

"We were in the darkness on the other side…"

But Brimir was unable to finish the sentence. Jolly-Goodday picked up his loudspeaker.

"Time for a joke!"

He brayed so loud their ears began to pop.

"What's brown and says 'Bee Gee'?"

"WHAT?" could be heard in unison from the flying children.

"A brown Bee-Gee! Ha Ha Ha **Ha Ha** Ha **Ha** Ha **Ha!"**

Jolly-Goodday lay in the sand, splitting his sides with laughter.

"We really must speak to the others," said Hulda, nudging Jolly-Goodday with her toe.

Jolly-Goodday was astonished.

"Why do you need to talk? Don't you want more fun and more jokes?"

"We have to tell the kids something important."

Jolly-Goodday handed Hulda the loudspeaker and she shouted into the air:

"Guys! Come here, we need to talk to you."

"We can't come right now, it's so dull if we stop flying. Tell us a joke!"

Hulda called out to them again, but the kids wouldn't listen.

"I know how to deal with these kiddyflies," said Jolly-Goodday, taking the loudspeaker.

"If you don't come right now I'll have the fierce wolf eat you!"

The children hurried down from the sky and gathered in a large group in front of Jolly-Goodday.

"And about time too," said Jolly-Goodday.

For the first time Brimir and Hulda now saw the faces of their friends again, and what Jolly-Goodday had said was true. Gray was indisputably in fashion. Everyone had become gray-haired. Magni's black hair was turned wolf-gray, and Elva's brown hair was as gray as dust.

"I thought it was our adventure in the darkness that had made us gray-haired, but why are they gray-haired too?" whispered Brimir to Hulda.

"They wish to talk to us," said Jolly-Goodday, pointing at Hulda and Brimir.

"Oh, we don't want any talking, except if we get more fun and games in return."

"They'll be very quick," said Jolly-Goodday.

Brimir and Hulda told the kids the whole story of the sun. How they had been blown into the darkness on the other side of the planet where the forest was blacker than coffee, and how they narrowly escaped from bears and hairy spiders thanks to the Teflon® wonder stuff.

"Hooray for Jolly-Goodday and Teflon® wonder stuff, which saved Hulda's and Brimir's lives," shouted the children. "Now can we go?"

"We haven't finished our story yet."

Brimir and Hulda told their friends about the home delivery service of the wild animals, and they told them about Darrow in the hyena's mouth, and about the poor pale children who were dying from hunger and cold sitting in the darkness waiting for the sun.

"Glad you're both back anyway," said the children. "Let's carry on flying, ha ha ha ha ha."

Brimir held out both his arms and stopped them.

"Didn't you hear our story, kids?"

"Yes, thanks, it was fun, ha ha ha ha ha."

"But what about the children in the darkness who are starving and shivering with cold in a dying forest? Shouldn't we help them?"

The kids shrugged their shoulders.

"How can we help them?" asked Elva innocently. "We're only children."

"Somebody must do something sometime," said Woody decisively, "but right now I'm missing out on some great flying time."

"Don't you care about the children in the darkness?"

"Are they also gray-haired?" asked Elva.

"No, they've just got ordinary hair," said Hulda.

The kids burst out laughing.

"How awful! Don't they keep up with the latest fashion?"

"Weren't you listening to what we were saying? They're dying," cried Hulda.

"Do you know what to do?" asked Woody, "I can't think of anything."

"I think it's best if we remove the nail from the sun," said Brimir.

One could hear a pin drop, the sound of feathers falling.

"REMOVE THE NAIL FROM THE SUN?" asked the children, gaping.

"Remove the nail from the sun?" asked Jolly-Goodday, gaping.

"And we must stop the wolf from chasing all the boring clouds over onto the other side of the planet," said Hulda.

"And we must let the butterflies fly again," said Brimir.

"Are you crazy?" asked the children. "Do you want us to die of boredom?"

"Otherwise the children on the other side will die of hunger in the cold and dark."

"You believe us, don't you, Jolly-Goodday?" asked Brimir. "You'll know how to save the children in the darkness. You have the answer to everything."

Who Owns the Sun?

Jolly-Goodday stood on the beach with a kindly smile. He patted Brimir on the head.

"Oh, my poor dears, I'd forgotten you are such little children and see things in such a simplistic way. You all think it's great fun to fly, don't you?"

"Yes," said the children.

"Isn't it more fun than anything else?"

"Ye-e-es!"

"And who taught you to fly?"

"You did, Jolly-Goodday."

"And who wanted to fly?"

"We wanted to fly, it was our most treasured dream."

"And the butterflies are on your land?"

"Our land? Is it possible to own land?"

"Yes, you own the land where the butterflies live and that's why you may do what you want with the butterflies. And if the others want to see the butterflies fly over their land then they must pay for it, because you own the butterflies. You're not going to stop flying unless they pay you to."

"Pay us? With what?"

"They can pay with gold."

"What do you do with gold?"

"You store it where no one else can see it."

The children thought this very strange.

"And what about the sun? Who owns the sun? It didn't start anywhere and never stops shining anywhere, but goes ring after ring and shines equally on all of the planet; that is until we had it fastened down with a nail," said Brimir.

"You own the sun, of course. The idea to nail down the sun was ours and if the others want the sun for a few days a year, then they'll have to pay for it."

The children thought about this for quite a while.

"In other words, the children on the other side really owe us gold for having been able to see the butterflies for free for hundreds of years," said Arnar the thinker.

"Exactly," said Jolly-Goodday. "Don't you think that's fair?"

Brimir and Hulda looked a little bewildered.

"We don't quite understand," they said. "That can't be right."

Jolly-Goodday heaved a sigh.

"I'll explain it to you in baby talk, since you're being so stupid. Do you want to stop flying and have everything as boring as it was in the old days?"

"No," mumbled everyone except Hulda and Brimir, who shuffled their feet uneasily.

"Do you remember how boring it was here before I came?"

"Yes, it was deadly dull."

"And do you remember what Hulda and Brimir said when I landed here?"

"They said you were a horrible man-eating space monster with fourteen heads and ten ears and sharp tusks."

"You see how they let their imagination run away with them? I turned out not to be a monster but the highly amusing Jolly-Goodday, and the children on the other side are definitely nowhere near as badly off as Brimir says they are, even though the sun is fixed above us. The children on the other side have the moon and stars."

"But the clouds the wolf drives away from us hide the stars and the moon on the other side," cried Brimir.

"Do you hear that, kids? The children on the other side have the moon and stars and all the clouds, and we have only the sun. And now what do they want? They want to have the sun for half a day too! What nerve!"

Brimir and Hulda protested.

"But the children on the other side live in eternal darkness!"

"And what did you tell the children on the other side?"

There was a long silence before Hulda muttered, "We told the children on the other side that there was eternal darkness here too."

"And that we looked so brown because we ate only soil," added Brimir.

"Did you hear that, kids? They told the children in the

darkness that we live in darkness, and then they tell us that there's darkness there. What can we believe? Are they perhaps always lying? First they see a space monster, then they see children in darkness. If I hadn't given them the Teflon® wonder stuff and butterfly powder, Brimir and Hulda would've been eaten by wild animals. Unless, of course, that was a lie too. And they call this gratitude!"

Jolly-Goodday had become really annoyed.

"There seems to be only one way to solve this problem. We must vote on it."

"Vote?"

"Then we'll know what the majority wants, and the majority is always right and should decide whether or not everything should continue to be fun. That's only fair, isn't it? Or maybe you two want to rule all on your own?"

"No, the majority must be right," said Brimir and Hulda.

The Elections

The kids looked at Hulda and Brimir who looked dejectedly down at the ground. Jolly-Goodday began to speak:

"My dear kids, before you vote I'm going to tell the truth once and for all. Although the sun is always on our side of the planet there is as much sunshine on the planet, on average, according to an index-calculated aggregate year, while bearing in mind the reported latest figures from the development process, which are within a 2% repository of bull and blarney, and when multiplied forty-five times and subtracted from the irritating hot air bull aspect of price equalizing regulatory procedures . . ."

"Hee, hee, I can't understand a word he's saying," giggled a little girl.

"Oh, my poor little thing, you are so silly," said Jolly-Goodday, patting her on the head. You don't have to understand me, you just have to believe and trust me. Look up at the blue sky. Listen to the birds. See the golden sun and the red apples and the green trees. Everything is fine the way it is! The island has never been more beautiful!"

Jolly-Goodday continued:

"If you want to keep up the same fun and games then we must fully utilize the sun. We must not remove the nail from it. There's as much happiness in the world now as there was previously, it's just been readjusted. We get just a bit MORE happiness, and the children on the other side of the planet get just a little less happiness."

"But the forest on the other side is dying and the children too," said Brimir. "We mustn't let that happen. Magni, you believe us, don't you?"

"Ha ha ha, huh, hm. Maybe Brimir has a point," said Magni cautiously. "Perhaps we should help the children on the other side."

Jolly-Goodday yawned.

"I can of course remove the nail and fix the sun again on the other side of the planet. It's the easiest thing in the world to do."

"Then we'd end up in everlasting darkness and cold!" shouted the children.

"That's none of my concern. The children on the other side will certainly want to have a fun time if you don't."

"But the kids on the other side would never let us end up in everlasting darkness," said Elva.

There was a long silence.

"Well, kids, do you think this is fun right now?" asked Jolly-Goodday.

"No, we want to get back to flying as soon as possible," answered most of them.

"Are you going to let Brimir and Hulda spoil all the fun for you? There will never be any fun again if the nail is removed from the sun, not to mention if you return the butterfly powder. Hurry up and vote so that you can carry on flying."

Hulda was on the verge of tears.

"Guys! Don't let him fool you. He doesn't care about the children in the darkness. He doesn't want to save them. He just talks his way out of things with glib tricks."

The children looked straight at Jolly-Goodday. Surely he didn't want the children in the darkness to die?

Jolly-Goodday put on a very sad expression.

"I most truly want to help the children in the darkness. It's precisely Brimir and Hulda who don't want to help them. They want to have *ME* remove the nail from the sun and let the children in the darkness fend for themselves."

"What do you want to do?" asked Brimir dejectedly.

"If we all pull together and send the children in the darkness food and blankets and shoes, then we'll save their lives and we can still keep the nail in the sun. Then everyone will be happy!"

"Wow, how clever Jolly-Goodday is," said the children.

But Brimir persisted with his argument.

"And what happens when they've finished all the food we send them?"

"Then we'll save them again and again and again . . ."

"That's really neat," said the children. "You're not only incredibly clever, but also terribly kind."

Jolly-Goodday smiled affectionately.

"Then let's vote on it now. It's your choice, dear children. If you vote for Brimir and Hulda then everything will be dull and boring again. If you vote for me the fun and games continue and we save the lives of the children on the other side of the planet."

And so the election began. The children received little ballot papers on which they had to choose who was right: Brimir and Hulda or Jolly-Goodday. The kids thought for a moment and placed their votes in the ballot box. The votes were counted and Jolly-Goodday announced the results, calling them out through the loudspeaker:

"More than one hundred children want to keep the nail in the sun, fly in the blue sky with butterfly powder on their hands, be coated with Teflon® wonder stuff, and save the children on the other side of the planet by sending them food, blankets, and shoes.

"Two want to return the butterfly powder, remove the nail from the sun, and have everything be BORING again.

"We know exactly who they are."

"Hooray," shouted the children. "More flying, more fun!"

Brimir looked at his friend Magni, who looked away. Brimir's eyes filled with tears. Hulda wanted to comfort him, but they were so slippery from the Teflon® wonder stuff that she couldn't hug him or hold his hands. Then Hulda's eyes filled with tears too.

"Come with me," she said to Brimir, sobbing.

They walked along the river and came to the waterfall, which trickled into the canyon without any sound of a roar or any spray splashing upwards to help form a rainbow in the gorge. They pealed off the Teflon® wonder stuff from their bodies and threw it into the waterfall. They then held hands and hugged and watched while a tiny little spray formed and a low roar could be heard from the canyon and a tiny rainbow appeared in the mist, though still a hundred times smaller than the old one.

"I'd forgotten how good it was to hold hands," said Brimir, smiling at Hulda.

They walked hand in hand up to the butterfly mountain and carefully peeped in through the cave opening. There slept the unsuspecting butterflies. The children dusted the butterfly powder off their hands and sprinkled it gently over a few butterfly wings. They then crept away and fell asleep in the shade of an oak tree.

The Rescue Party

While Brimir and Hulda slept under a tree, a tremendous rescue party was held on Black Beach to celebrate the election results. A barrel was to be filled with blankets and food and then thrown into the sea so that it would float over to the children on the other side of the planet and save their lives.

"You don't have to be sore losers and cry-babies like Hulda and Brimir, who don't understand that the majority always knows best," said Jolly-Goodday. "We can cheer up the children on the other side of the planet much better than they can."

"Hooray! Let's cheer up the children in the darkness," shouted the children in one voice.

Jolly-Goodday rolled a barrel out of his spaceship, emptying some candy wrappers out of it first. He stood it up on the beach.

"When we've filled this barrel, we'll roll it out into the sea and it will float over to the pale hungry children."

The children hovered above the barrel.

"I don't need these shoes when I'm always flying," said Magni, throwing his old shoes into the barrel.

"And I don't need a blanket as there's always sunshine," said Elva, throwing her blanket into the barrel.

"And I can't finish this apple," said Woody, and he threw the remains of the apple into the barrel.

Then they all ate as much as they could stuff themselves with. But at the height of the party some strange objects appeared on the horizon.

"What are they?" asked the children, staring out to sea.

Jolly-Goodday picked up his telescope and looked out over the ocean.

"They're crates and rafts. They must be coming out of the darkness on the other side of the planet!"

Jolly-Goodday looked at the children and frowned.

"I've traveled far and wide and seen many things, but I've never seen anything as serious as this. This is clearly an invading army. WAR has been declared!"

"**WAR?** What's that?"

"War is when someone gets into such a bad temper that he turns the smell of the volcanoes and the iron in the mountains into bombs, which he then throws at everyone he doesn't like."

"Are the children on the other side now angry with us?"

"They've found out who stole the sun and the butterflies from them and sent them darkness and clouds instead."

"So are the children in the darkness going to kill us?"

"That's how it goes when there's a war," said Jolly-Goodday, shrugging his shoulders.

The waves carried the crates with the invading force closer and closer to Black Beach. The children dashed to and fro in confusion.

"We must drive the invaders back!"

"Quick, Jolly-Goodday, make some bombs from the smell of volcanoes and the iron in the mountains."

"Yes, quickly!" shouted the children. "We must blow them up before it's too late!"

Jolly-Goodday thought it over. The first crates had almost reached the shoreline.

"It's a little bit expensive," said Jolly-Goodday calmly.

"How much does a bomb cost?" shouted the children.

"It will cost one heart per person to throw a bomb," said Jolly-Goodday.

"One heart?"

"It's impossible to throw bombs if you have a normal child's heart in your breast. As soon as you throw a bomb it becomes either a stone heart or a steel heart."

"And how would that change us?"

"You won't grow any bigger and you won't get any smaller, but if you get a stone heart your life will be much easier, you won't even need to have friends."

"What about a steel heart?"

"Then you'll never be bored and never be happy and

won't need to have feelings anymore. Men with steel hearts never cry."

"Quick, Jolly-Goodday, save us. Make the bombs!"

Jolly-Goodday transformed the smell of volcanoes and the iron in the mountains into bombs, which he handed out to the children. He then took cover behind a rock and hunched down with the loudspeaker. The children took their places on the shoreline and aimed at the invading army on the sea.

Ready, aim, and BOMBS AWAY!" bellowed Jolly-Goodday.

But there was no explosion. The children held onto their bombs as no one wanted to be the first to throw one. No one liked the idea of getting a stone heart or a steel heart. Jolly-Goodday picked up his loudspeaker and shouted at the children:

"Are you complete wimps? You'll be utterly defeated in this war if you don't throw the bombs! Hurry up before it's too late!"

The invading rafts had come right up to the land and at last a wave caught hold of one of them and smashed it to pieces, spilling its contents all over the beach. The children looked on in amazement.

"It isn't an invincible invading army! It's a pile of blankets!"

"They've clearly planned the attack very carefully,"

said Jolly-Goodday. "They've sent supplies ahead of them. You should blow up the next crate. **Ready, aim, BOMBS AWAY!"**

But no one threw a bomb. The waves caught hold of more and more crates and broke them open along the shoreline. Out of them tumbled shoes, clothes, blankets, and potatoes or dried fish.

The children stood speechless on the beach as the waves threw the last crate ashore. It landed without breaking open and the children crept all round it.

"What is it?"

"Be careful," said Jolly-Goodday. "It could be a nuclear bomb."

The Bomb in the Crate

Magni crept up to the crate and carefully broke open the lid.

"What is it?" asked the children.

Magni remained silent.

"Magni, what is it?"

"Just papers."

"What's written on them?"

"Death threats?"

"Declarations of war?"

"Ultimatums?"

Magni flipped through the pile of papers.

"They're stories."

"Stories?"

"Yes, they're fairy tales and sagas, and poems too."

"Poems?"

"And there's a letter."

"Read it."

Dear children

We hope you are still alive. We met your friends Hulda and Brimir the other day and they told us what a very hard time you've been having since the sun disappeared. We hope they got home in the air balloon which we gave them. Because your darkness is even blacker than ours we really wanted to help make your lives a little more bearable, and that's why we've sent you food and blankets and stories and poems, so you won't have to eat soil or get bored.

Best wishes,
The children by the firefly jar.

"Are the children in the darkness sending us food?" asked the children, and they looked at the bombs in their hands.

Jolly-Goodday burst out laughing.

"Ha ha ha ha!!! They are so stupid!" he shouted and rolled about laughing. "They believed what Brimir and Hulda told them! They think that you're so hungry you eat nothing but soil!"

No one laughed except for a few who giggled self-consciously.

"They're sending us blankets and poems?" asked the children.

Jolly-Goodday laughed even more, bringing tears to his eyes.

"Ha ha! I've never heard anything like it! They are in the darkness and cold and send blankets and food over to the sun and warmth, because they think there's darkness here too."

"Why are they so kind to us?" asked the children.

"I don't know," said Jolly-Goodday. "Some people just are so stupid and gullible."

The children stood on the shoreline and stared at the barrel they were planning to float over to the pale children. Flies buzzed all around it as food, blankets, and old shoes were all mixed together.

"Okay now, carry on flying, kids, and let's forget all this. Ready, steady, off you go."

No one moved.

"What's the matter with you all?"

No one answered.

"Kids who live in the cold and darkness and give away blankets and rainbow trout must be so stupid that they don't deserve to have the sun where they live," said Jolly-Goodday. "They wouldn't know what to do with it. Get on flying now."

The children stood on the beach with drooping heads. Elva was going to embrace Magni, but he was too slippery.

"Come with me," said Elva, nudging Magni.

Magni nudged Woody, who nudged Arnar, who nudged the next child, and they all glided up to Fairmost Falls. They landed by the waterfall, which trickled

like saliva down into the canyon. The children peeled off the Teflon® magic coating and threw it into the waterfall.

The spray increased as more and more of the children threw the stuff into the waterfall, and its roar became louder and louder until the thunder was almost deafening. In fact, it was so deafening that all the jokes Jolly-Goodday had ever told the children were totally forgotten. And then a large and beautiful rainbow formed over the canyon.

The children closed their eyes and felt the spray caress their bodies. They then flapped up to Mount Bright and dusted the butterfly powder carefully over the butterflies. The children embraced and kissed each other and then walked back. Many of them soon became very tired, as they hadn't used their legs since the sun had been nailed to the sky. Their bones were weak, their joints stiff, and some of them walked with a stick.

When they at last reached the beach Jolly-Goodday stood all alone on the shoreline folding up his deck chair.

"Ignorant, ungrateful children," he muttered. "I'm leaving!"

"Why have we become so old and weak?" asked the children.

"You sold me your youth for more fun."

"But now the fun's over, can't we have our youth back?"

"It's mine now. You sold me your youth and I'll decide what I'm going to do with it."

"What are you going to do with our youth? We don't want to be gray-haired and weary."

"Youth is the most precious stuff in the world. It's more valuable than gold or diamonds and it fuels my spaceship. With your youth I should be able to reach the next solar system, and if I have any youth left I can buy myself lots of friends."

"Don't you have any friends?" asked the children. Jolly-Goodday didn't answer, and they looked sadly at him. The spaceship's fuel tank was almost full.

"Are you going to use our youth as fuel and money?"

"Are you going to leave us so old and gray-haired?"

"But you think it's cool to be gray-haired, it's in fashion," said Jolly-Goodday and he picked up his loudspeaker:

"Once upon a time there was a woman who had a dog called Latest Fashion but it got lost while she was in the shower and the woman ran out onto her balcony stark naked and cried out: 'Latest Fashion! Latest Fashion!' And after that everyone walked around stark naked because they thought it was the latest fashion."

No one laughed at the joke.

"Will you please give us our youth back?" asked Elva gently.

"But my spaceship runs on youth. Perhaps you'd rather I stayed here?"

No one answered.

"Are you going to remove the nail from the sun first?"

"I don't do anything for ungrateful children."

"But only you can remove the nail from the sun," said the children. "It must be removed otherwise the children on the other side will die."

"It'll cost you to have the nail removed from the sun, kids."

"How much?"

"Only a single drop of youth from one child's heart."

"Pooh, that's not much, how much youth do we have left?"

"There's exactly a single drop in each heart."

"You're mad! The last drop is irremovable from the heart!"

"You can easily get a heart of stone to replace it," said Jolly-Goodday.

"But one little drop can't make any difference, you've already got a full tank."

"The last drop is the most valuable of all. A dying king on another planet would give his kingdom for the last drop from a child's heart."

"We can't let you have the last drop!" shouted the children. "We'd rather die than get a stone heart."

"It's up to you," said Jolly-Goodday. "Either one of you receives a stone heart or all the stupid children on the other side of the planet will die in the darkness."

"You *are* a space monster," said the children.

"Aren't you the ones who wanted to have fun at night and nail the sun in the sky?"

"Yes."

"And aren't you the ones who voted not to remove the nail from the sun?"

"Yes."

"The majority is always right and I only did what the majority wanted. I'm no monster, you're the monsters. You voted to let the children in the darkness remain in the darkness. It seems to me you already have stone hearts in your breasts."

No one answered.

"If someone will volunteer to give me their last drop of youth I'll remove the nail from the sun and everything will be as it was before. Otherwise I'm out of here."

Jolly-Goodday stepped into his spaceship and was about to zoom away and burn up all their youth while jetting far away into space where other planets awaited him.

But then a voice was heard from the crowd of children.

"You may have my last drop if you remove the nail from the sun."

The children gasped in amazement. It was Brimir who had spoken.

Steel-hearted or Stone-hearted

The children stood silently and stared at Brimir.

Jolly-Goodday stepped down from his spaceship and smiled.

"That was a wise decision."

No one said anything as Brimir stepped to the front of the group.

"You promise to remove the nail from the sun when you have taken the last drop of my youth?"

"I promise. Haven't I always stood by my word?" said Jolly-Goodday smiling broadly.

No one else smiled.

"Which do you prefer, a steel heart or a stone heart?"

Brimir regarded the children and thought it over. If he received a stone heart he wouldn't need any friends. If he received a steel heart he would be indifferent to everything.

"I don't want any heart in exchange," he said. "I'd rather die than have a stone heart or a steel heart."

"I'm not an evil man, I don't want to kill you," said Jolly-Goodday. "I'll give you a stone heart. They don't want to be your friends anyway."

Jolly-Goodday pressed a button on the side of the spaceship and an operating table descended with a loud crash. He pressed another button and a little mechanical drill appeared along with a vacuum cleaner. He pulled a lever on the operating table and an umbrella and a sewing machine popped up.

"It's a simple operation," explained Jolly-Goodday. "I open and close the umbrella very rapidly and this in turn drives the drill, which saws a small hole in your chest. The vacuum cleaner then sucks the old heart out of you and squirts a stone heart into the wound, after which the sewing machine takes over and you'll be as good as new!"

Brimir looked over his shoulder to his friends. After the operation he would be cold and emotionless and without need of them. He looked for Hulda but could not find her. Oh, he so wanted to embrace her for the last time. He lay down on the operating table and closed his eyes. Jolly-Goodday took up his position and vigorously started to open and close the umbrella. The drill began to whine and descended closer and closer . . .

Veeeeeeeeeeeeee.

Jolly-Goodday's Dream

But suddenly there was a shout.

"Wait a minute, Jolly-Goodday! Wait a minute!"

Everyone looked around. It was Hulda.

"What now?" asked Jolly-Goodday, closing the umbrella. "Can't you see I'm busy?"

"What do you dream of, Jolly-Goodday?" asked Hulda.

"Wh- wh- what do you mean? What do I dream?"

"What do you dream of?" asked Hulda again, and she looked him straight in the eyes.

"Why do you ask?"

"Answer me."

Jolly-Goodday looked embarassed.

"I don't know. I make other people's dreams come true and have no interest in my own."

"Don't you ever dream?"

Jolly-Goodday muttered, "Yes, sometimes I dream."

"About what?" asked Hulda.

Jolly-Goodday shuffled his feet, running his toe in the sand.

"About being a king," he murmured.

"What?"

"I want to be a king," said Jolly-Goodday a little louder.

The children looked at him and started whispering to each other. A king? Was that all? Was that his dearest wish? Some of them couldn't resist laughing. How extraordinary.

Jolly-Goodday looked with distant eyes into space and seemed to have lost himself in his dream.

"I dream of being a king in a castle with a moat full of crocodiles and a large throne and a drawbridge and a high tower from which I can see over my kingdom and shout orders to my subjects."

The children were completely amazed.

"Were you taking our youth and making us gray-haired just because you wanted to be a king in a faraway kingdom?"

"I was hoping to sell the last drop of youth on a planet where the king is very old in exchange for my being king in his place."

"Tell us some more about your dream," said Hulda, hoping they would gain time to save Brimir's heart.

Jolly-Goodday closed his eyes and talked and talked about crowns and jewels and beautiful horses and how he could ride in a coach around his kingdom and wave to his subjects with his mace.

The children listened gobsmacked.

"Guys, we have to find a way to save Brimir," whispered Hulda.

The children gathered together while Jolly-Goodday still had his eyes closed and rambled on and on . . .

"The castle would be covered in seashells and diamonds . . ."

"I've got an idea that always works in fairy tales," said Magni. "We have to kill Jolly-Goodday. Just like trolls and dragons and witches are killed in fairy tales."

"Exactly," said Elva. "A troll woman is turned to stone in sunlight, witches are roasted in ovens, dragons are slain with swords."

"We must kill him and save Brimir," all the children agreed. "We should attack him all at once."

The children got themselves ready to attack Jolly-Goodday.

"No, no! He mustn't be killed," said Hulda decisively.

"Why not? He's evil."

"Yes, he's a space monster."

"But he only did what we asked him to do. He granted our wishes and if he dies we'll never get the nail out of the sun and the children in the darkness will die too."

"What do you want to do?"

"I've a much better idea," said Hulda. "Now listen carefully."

Hulda took a deep breath and looked seriously at her friends.

"We shall make Jolly-Goodday a king and make his dream come true, just like he made our dreams come true."

The children looked at her in amazement.

"ARE YOU CRAZY?" whispered Elva. "This man is very dangerous. We should put him in prison instead."

The children looked at Jolly-Goodday where he stood by the operating table, his eyes closed, and a joyful look on his face: "And everybody would bow to me . . ."

"Hulda, you've gone mad. We can't let just anybody be a king," whispered the children.

"Don't you get it?" whispered Hulda in reply. "A king is like a monkey in a cage. You just have to feed him and have fun watching him, but otherwise you won't have to worry about him."

Jolly-Goodday continued to talk about his dream. "And I could look over the land and say: this is my kingdom."

"We must lock him up in prison," said the children to Hulda.

"No," said Hulda. "It's easier to lock him up in a castle."

Jolly-Goodday had still not finished. "And I'd have a gold crown on my head."

Hulda continued, "It's also much more fun to build a castle than a prison."

"But a king rules over everything! We can't let him rule over us!"

"A king rules over grown-ups. We are wild children and can do what we like."

"But how do we get our youth back?"

"I know how," said Hulda.

The children looked at each other and then at Brimir where he lay on the operating table between the umbrella and the sewing machine, waiting for whatever would happen.

Hulda cried out, "Jolly-Goodday!"

He came out of his trance and stopped talking about his dream.

"What?"

"You can be king."

His Majesty Jolly-Goodday

Jolly-Goodday was dumbfounded.

"What? What do you mean, I can be king?"

"You can be king with a crown and a castle with a moat and crocodiles."

Jolly-Goodday looked disbelievingly at the children.

"Are you telling the truth?"

"Yes," said the children. "You may be king of the island and us and all the animals."

"I can hardly believe it," said Jolly-Goodday, and tears appeared in his eyes.

"You'll be king of the sun and the clouds and the moon and the stars and the butterflies."

"Really?"

"Scouts' honor!" said the children.

Jolly-Goodday's face was a picture of joy.

"But why do you want to make my dream come true?"

"You made our dreams come true, so of course it's only polite to make your dreams come true too."

"Am I king now?"

"Yes, you may start giving orders. Henceforth you bear the title His Majesty Jolly-Goodday."

Jolly-Goodday smiled broadly as he disappeared into his spaceship. When he reappeared he was wearing black leather boots and a wine-red robe, with a gold crown on his head and a massive gold mace in his hand.

"It just so happens I had all this in a cupboard," said Jolly-Goodday, blushing a little.

And then with a look of concentration he began to rule.

"Subjects! You must build a castle for me."

But the children looked woefully tired.

"We can't. See how gray-haired, old, and weak we are? We'd take no time at all to build the nicest castle in the world if we only had more youth in our hearts."

"How much do you need?"

"Just a few drops. Hardly worth mentioning," said the children.

"That's no problem, kids. I've got a full tank of youth."

Jolly-Goodday walked pompously to his spaceship, though with a very strange gait. He clearly wanted to hop and skip all the way. He passed Brimir who still lay on the operating table.

"Subject! Why are you lying there like a stranded jelly-fish? Aren't you supposed to be building a castle?"

Brimir was so surprised he could only stammer.

"Oh, you poor thing, you're too weak to speak."

Jolly-Goodday dipped a ladle into the tank of youth and gave Brimir a good drink. Brimir could feel youth surge through every vein and nerve before it entered his heart. Jolly-Goodday gave the other children a few drops as well, and their faces became smoother, their legs stronger, and part of their gray hair became blond or black or red.

Everyone gave a helping hand and before long a giant white castle rose on the beach, with towers and a moat full of crocodiles. Jolly-Goodday glowed with happiness and went straight up to the highest tower to look out over his kingdom.

"Now I need stable boys and a stable!" he cried.

"You don't need either a stable or stable boys," cried the children in reply. "The horses take care of themselves and feed on the grass in the meadow."

"But who will fetch them for me?"

"They'll come if you call to them."

"What a clever system," said Jolly-Goodday, and he smiled. Then he became thoughtful again.

"I need servants and cooks!" he cried.

"No need," said the children. "The fruit trees grow right up to your windows and you can reach out for pineapples or apples or oranges whenever you're hungry."

"And penguins lay their eggs in the palace courtyard. You can fry them."

"And if I want meat?"

"Seals sleep on the beach. You can knock out a seal with your mace. You don't want servants to use your mace, do you?" asked Hulda.

"No, I couldn't allow that," said Jolly-Goodday. "I use it to rule with."

"And kings so enjoy hunting birds and deer and salmon. You don't want servants to be doing that for you?"

"That's true," said Jolly-Goodday. "Only kings should hunt deer and salmon, not serving folk."

Jolly-Goodday had yet another thought.

"But I need guards and soldiers," he cried.

"We're all such good friends that you don't need soldiers," said the children.

"That's a clever idea," said Jolly-Goodday. "I hadn't thought of that."

Jolly-Goodday had another brainwave.

"But a chest of gold. Someone must make a chest and look for gold in the mountain and dig it up so it can be kept in the gold vault under my castle."

"But you're the king of the mountain and it's much safer to keep the gold where no one knows where it is. Then you can be sure no one could ever find it."

"What another clever system," replied Jolly-Goodday. "I'm certainly the wisest and cleverest king in the world."

The children smiled at each other and then

Jolly-Goodday had another thought and called out of his tower window, "But where am I to keep the rest of the youth? The tank in the spaceship could rust and disintegrate after I've moved into the castle."

"You're king over us so it will be by far the safest to keep youth in the deep well of our hearts. Then there'll be more than a hundred subjects safeguarding it."

Jolly-Goodday beamed.

"That's a brilliantly good idea. Then no one can take it from you."

Jolly-Goodday let the children have all their youth back and the wells in their hearts were as full as they had been before. Their skins were as smooth as a baby's bottom and their hair as yellow as a sandy beach, as black as a raven, or as red as fire. The children were smiling from ear to ear in the sunshine, but Brimir was still worried.

"What about the children in the darkness?" he whispered.

"Don't worry," said Hulda. "Isn't everything perfect now, Jolly-Goodday?"

Jolly-Goodday thought and thought. At last he called out through the window, "Everything's perfect!"

"Aren't you king of the moon and stars and clouds?" asked Hulda.

"Yes, I most certainly am," said Jolly-Goodday.

"But how can you keep an eye on the moon and stars when the sun is fixed with a nail over the island, and how can you see your clouds when the wolf drives them away?"

Jolly-Goodday had a good think about that.

"I must remove the nail from the sun and kill the wolf," said Jolly-Goodday. "Then I'll be able to see the moon and stars and clouds."

Jolly-Goodday was delighted over this brilliant plan of his.

"I'm undoubtedly the wisest king who has ever ruled over this island."

Jolly-Goodday went out into the palace courtyard and shouted up into the air, **"WOLF! WOLF! COME HERE RIGHT NOW!"**

Then came the most awful growl that had ever been heard as the wolf shot across the sky and hovered over them. Jolly-Goodday took out his most powerful vacuum cleaner and pointed it at the wolf so that it was sucked up the tube. Then only a faint howl could be heard from within the vacuum cleaner. And since that day a faint howling moan can always be heard within vacuum cleaners.

"Hooray for Jolly-Goodday!" shouted the children.

Quite soon clouds started coming cautiously over the island again. Some were like woolly lambs and others like flying swans, and many like camels that keep water in their humps. Jolly-Goodday took out his long ladder and rested it against a cloud that looked like a whale. His Majesty Jolly-Goodday climbed up into the sky with a gigantic crowbar and removed the nail from the sun.

"Hooray, the sun's free!" shouted the children.

Now the day was no longer permanent. The sun continued its journey across the sky and disappeared at last beyond the horizon. The kids strained their ears.

"Sssh . . ."

And at last they all heard the sound they had been waiting for. From far in the distance, they first heard a cry of amazement, and then an unbelievable shout of joy.

"HOORAY! HOORAY! HOORAY!"

The cheering carried from the dark side of the blue planet, which was now no longer dark. The children there were welcoming the sun for the first time in a long time.

"Now the children in the darkness will be happy," said Hulda smiling. "Because now they're the children in the light."

The moon rose and lit up the stars. Then the voice of his majesty Jolly-Goodday could be heard from his tower window:

"Subjects! Is no one going to amuse me?"

The children sat on the beach around a campfire and recited to each other poems or fairy tales about space monsters.

"We're not important enough to step inside the palace," cried Hulda.

"Come and join us by the fire, we'll tell you fairy tales," said Brimir.

His Majesty Jolly-Goodday came and sat with the children by the fire. They told him stories and fairy tales all night, and he told them about the distant stars he had visited. They then all fell asleep in the warm sand by the fire and dreamed amazing dreams. When the children woke up the next day, the air was full of fluttering butterflies in thousands of colors. No one said a word except Jolly-Goodday, who just smiled and whispered:

"Oh, what delightful beauty."

ANDRI SNÆR MAGNASON is one of Iceland's most celebrated young writers. In 2002 *LoveStar* was named "Novel of the Year" by Icelandic booksellers and received the DV Literary Award and a nomination to the Icelandic Literary Prize. *The Story of the Blue Planet*—now published or performed in 22 countries—was the first children's book to receive the Icelandic Literary Prize and was also the recipient of the Janusz Korczak Honorary Award and the West Nordic Children's Book Prize. Andri is the winner of the 2010 Kairos Award.

ÁSLAUG JÓNSDÓTTIR is an illustrator, author of children's books, artist, and graphic designer. She has written and illustrated several books for children, amongst them *The Egg* (*Eggið*, 2003), *I Want Fish!* (*Ég vil fisk!* 2007), and the award-winning *Good Evening* (*Gott kvöld*, 2005), which received The Bookseller's Prize as the best children's book of 2005, The Icelandic Illustration Award, The Reykjavik Educational Council Children's Book Prize, and was nominated for The Nordic Children's Book Award.

JULIAN MELDON D'ARCY is Professor of English Literature at the University of Iceland. He has written books on Scottish literature and sports, and has translated novels, poetry, and films from Icelandic, including the children's books *Flowers on the Roof* and *The Fisherman's Boy and the Seal*.

PUSHKIN CHILDREN'S BOOKS

Just as we all are, children are fascinated by stories. From the earliest age, we love to hear about monsters and heroes, romance and death, disaster and rescue, from every place and time.

In 2013, we created Pushkin Children's Books to share these tales from different languages and cultures with younger readers, and to open the door to the wide, colourful worlds these stories offer.

From picture books and adventure stories to fairy tales and classics, and from fifty-year-old bestsellers to current huge successes abroad, the books on the Pushkin Children's list reflect the very best stories from around the world, for our most discerning readers of all: children.